Unleashed Praise for the
Barking Detective Mysteries

"Three woofs and a big bow-wow for *Dial C for Chihuahua*. Pepe is one cool sleuth—just don't call him a dog! I really loved the book."
—**Leslie Meier**, author of the Lucy Stone mysteries

"Readers will sit up and beg for more."
—**Sushi the Shih Tzu**, canine star of the *Trash 'n' Treasures* mysteries by Barbara Allan

"Writing duo Curtis has created a humorous but deadly serious mystery. Pepe is a delight and more intelligent than most humans in the book. An ex-husband and current love interest keep Geri's life hopping. Crafty plotting will keep you engrossed until the end and have you eagerly awaiting the next book."
—*RT Book Reviews*, 4 Stars

"Every dog has its day and there'll be plenty of days for Geri Sullivan and Pepe in this fun twist on the typical PI partnership."
—**Simon Wood**, author of *Did Not Finish*

"Waverly Curtis has created a delightful cast of human and canine characters in *Dial C for Chihuahua*. Pepe never loses his essential dogginess, even as he amazes gutsy Geri Sullivan, his partner in crime detection, with his past exploits and keen nose for detail. I look forward to Pepe's next adventure!"
—**Bernadette Pajer**, author of the Professor Bradshaw Mysteries

"Move over, Scooby-Doo, there's a new dog in town! *Dial C for Chihuahua* is a fun and breezy read, with polished writing and charming characters, both human and canine. If you like a little Chihuahua with your mystery, former purse-dog Pepe is a perfect fit!"
—**Jennie Bentley**, author of the Do-It-Yourself Home Renovation mysteries

Also by Waverly Curtis

*Dial C for Chihuahua**

*A Barking Detective Mystery

Chihuahua Confidential

Waverly Curtis

KENSINGTON PUBLISHING CORP.
http://www.kensingtonbooks.com

KENSINGTON BOOKS are published by

Kensington Publishing Corp.
119 West 40th Street
New York, NY 10018

All Kensington Titles, Imprints, and Distributed Lines are
available at special quantity discounts for bulk purchases
for sales promotions, premiums, fund-raising, and educa-
tional or institutional use.

Special book excerpts or customized printings can also
be created to fit specific needs. For details, write or
phone the office of the Kensington special sales manager:
Kensington Publishing Corp., 119 West 40th Street,
New York, NY 10018, attn: Special Sales Department,
Phone: 1-800-221-2647.

Kensington and the K logo Reg. U.S. Pat & TM Off.

ISBN-13: 978-0-7582-7496-0
ISBN-10: 0-7582-7496-3

First Mass Market Printing: April 2013

10 9 8 7 6 5 4 3 2 1

Printed in the United States of America

For Stephanie

Chapter 1

My counselor insisted I come in for an appointment before I left Seattle. She wanted to discuss my talking Chihuahua, Pepe.

I could totally understand her concerns. There were times when I questioned my own sanity.

Two hours after I adopted a cute white Chihuahua from a Seattle shelter, he started talking. And he hasn't stopped since. Even as we drove to the appointment, Pepe was chattering away about all the things he wanted to show me when we got to L.A.

He claimed he had once lived there, as the pampered pet of Caprice Kennedy, the ditzy blond starlet famous for her love of small dogs.

I really didn't believe this story. He had dozens of stories, all preposterous. He claimed to have fought a bull in Mexico City, raced in the Iditarod in Alaska, and wrestled an alligator in an Alabama swamp. It pained him that I didn't believe his stories. And I could appreciate that,

since no one believed me when I said my dog
talked.

If anyone was going to believe me, I had high
hopes for my counselor. Susanna is the sort of
woman who sees auras and talks about chakras.
Her waiting room is cluttered with crystals (to
channel energy) and overflowing with plants (to
detoxify the environment). She dyes her hair a
shocking shade of red and wears chunky jewelry.

"So, Geri," Susanna began, after waving me
and Pepe to a seat on the dark gray velour sofa
in her office, "is your dog still talking to you?"

"Of course I am still talking to her," said Pepe.
"Who else would I talk to? She is the only one
who can hear me."

"That's not true," I pointed out to him.
"There is one other person who can hear you."

"It is of little merit," Pepe said. "That *ladrón*
is in jail."

Susanna was quick to jump in. "So you believe
he spoke to you just then?"

"Yes," I said, "and he pointed out that we met
another person who could hear him talk."

"Oh, really?" Susanna asked. "I would like to
meet this person."

"Well, unfortunately, you can't," I said. Because the only other person who could hear
Pepe speak was a murderer. I had already told
Susanna about getting a job at a private detective
agency. Pepe had insisted on going with me to
my first appointment, where we stumbled over
the corpse of David Tyler.

Susanna looked disturbed. "That's quite a
story, Geri."

"You say that as if I made it up."

"Now you see what it is like when you scoff at my stories," said Pepe, with some satisfaction.

"I heard the police made an arrest in the Tyler case," Susanna said, "but they didn't mention you."

"What do you expect?" I asked. My counselor knows the story of my life. I've been going to her ever since she started seeing clients at the clinic associated with the college where she got her master's in counseling. The clinic offered a sliding scale, and I needed that after my divorce since I was only making enough money to make ends meet. So she knew that after I put my husband through business school, he left me for his secretary at his first job. And that just as my career as a stager was taking off, the real estate market crashed. I never get credit for my accomplishments.

"What does she mean, Geri?" Pepe asked. "Are we not heroes?"

My dog loves the limelight. Perhaps he once lived in Beverly Hills after all. It was theoretically possible since he was one of a group of Chihuahuas who had been flown up to Seattle because the shelters in Los Angeles were overflowing with them.

"The Seattle police wanted to take credit for the arrest," I said. Actually they had threatened to arrest me for practicing as a PI without a license.

"That is outrageous!" declared Pepe. "When it was I who felled the foe!"

"It's OK with me," I said. I really don't like

center stage. Which is why it was so annoying that my dog kept putting me right in the middle of the most ridiculous schemes. For instance, we were about to leave for L.A. to participate in the pilot episode of a reality TV show called *Dancing with Dogs*. Rebecca Tyler, David's widow, was producing it and said it was going to be a cross between *So You Think You Can Dance* and *Dancing with the Stars*. Pepe was thrilled but I was terrified.

"By the way, I'm going to have to cancel my appointment for next week. Pepe and I are going to be in L.A., filming a TV show."

Susanna shook her head. "You should be checking yourself into a hospital, not going on a trip."

Pepe, who had been lying down, sat up abruptly.

"No way, Geri!" said Pepe. "I need you as my partner." It was unclear whether he meant for dancing or for investigating. He has this delusion that we are partners in a detective agency called Sullivan and Sullivan.

"I can't abandon my dog," I said.

Susanna's eyes grew dark with worry. "Geri, this is all so unlike you. Stories about catching a murderer. An invitation to perform in a reality TV show. A sudden trip to L.A. Do you realize what this sounds like?"

"No," I said. "What does it sound like?"

"Mania," said Susanna.

"Fun!" said Pepe.

* * *

My dog, like most dogs, knows how to have fun. And there's something contagious about being around that kind of joy. Which may be why we adopt dogs in the first place.

And Pepe was definitely enjoying himself. He spent the two hours of the flight from Sea-Tac to LAX running around the private jet with Siren Song, the golden Pomeranian belonging to Rebecca Tyler, who had chartered the plane. Pepe and I met Rebecca after her husband was killed, and we helped her locate the missing money she needed to fund *Dancing with Dogs*. This was her pet project: a reality TV show featuring dog owners dancing with their pets for cash prizes. Rebecca spent most of the flight on her phone, talking with her casting director and her agent. She was busy trying to line up sponsors and celebrity judges for the show.

In the Los Angeles airport, everyone stared at our entourage. Rebecca looked stunning as usual, striding through the terminal in a chic black dress and sparkly high heels, with Siren Song trotting at one side, her hunky gardener-turned-bodyguard, Luis Montoya, at her other side, carrying her luggage.

I trailed behind with Pepe tucked in the crook of my elbow. I felt very self-conscious in an outfit that was perfect for Seattle's rainy climate—black jeans, a violet-colored sweater, and a black velvet jacket. It was apparently all wrong for L.A. Most of the women in the airport were wearing low-cut, brightly colored, tight tops and tiny skirts that showed off their long tan legs and strappy high heels. Their hair was sleek and styled and mostly blond (or highlighted if not blond) while mine was curly and messy and very dark. And their nails gleamed in various shades of red and pink and even orange. Mine were bitten down to the quick.

Still I held my head high as I passed through the gauntlet of their stares. I assume they thought I was Pepe's handler. He certainly acted like a star, gazing out over the crowds with a little smile on his lips and a proud tilt to his head.

"Ah, Los Angeles," he said. "The City of Angels."

A white Hummer limo was waiting for us at the curb and we settled in. Rebecca got back on the phone while Pepe positioned himself at the window, gazing out and keeping a running commentary on various landmarks we passed.

"There is Century City, Geri," he said, pointing out a cluster of skyscrapers. "I attended a big premiere there with Caprice. Those were the days when she took me everywhere with her. She dyed my fur to match her gown."

"Geri?" asked Rebecca. She and Siren Song and Luis were sitting in the back of the limousine, which was about half a mile from where we were sitting. "Is Pepe all right? He's making quite a racket."

"He's fine," I told her. I tend to forget that nobody can understand him but me. "He's just excited, Rebecca," I added. "For that matter, so am I."

"Well," she said with a smile, "you'll be even more excited when you find out who just agreed to be our last celebrity judge."

"Really?" I asked. "Who?"

"*Sí*, who?" asked Pepe, his long ears pricked forward.

"Caprice Kennedy!" Rebecca said, and she practically squealed, which is unusual for her, as she is one of the coolest characters you will ever see. She didn't even cry when she found out her husband was murdered.

"Yes," Rebecca continued. "Isn't it wonderful? Having such a famous movie star and dog lover on our show is going to guarantee that the networks will pick it up!"

"Dog lover," mumbled Pepe. "Or dog discarder."

Poor Pepe. Caprice had ditched him for another dog. I'd been ditched myself a few times and could understand how he was feeling.

"And she'll be meeting us at the hotel for a photo shoot," Rebecca went on.

"She will?"

"Yes. Isn't it exciting?"

"I wonder if she will remember me," Pepe said softly.

"Of course she will," I told him.

Rebecca leaned toward me. "It's great publicity for *Dancing with Dogs*. The best! And great publicity for Caprice, too. She needs it! After the troubles she's had. All those DUIs. That impulsive wedding in Las Vegas. Then dropping out of rehab. This will cast her in a much better light. That's part of the reason she agreed to be on the show. Her agent said as much when I talked to him."

"Caprice is young," said Pepe. "It is only natural for her to sow some wild oats."

"Why, Pepe," I said, "sounds to me like you still have a soft spot for her."

"Everyone makes mistakes," he told me.

"Wake up, Siren Song." Rebecca gave her sleeping Pomeranian a shake. "We're almost there, my little darling. You've got to be at your best."

The limousine rolled to a stop under a striped awning. Someone opened the door from the outside, and before I could stop him, Pepe hopped out.

"Pepe!" I jumped out after him, afraid he would run into traffic. He was always doing this to me, getting me into all sorts of predicaments. If it hadn't been for him running into Rebecca Tyler's house, I wouldn't have gotten mixed up in her husband's murder. On the other hand, if Pepe hadn't antagonized a Great Dane in a parking lot, I wouldn't have met the handsome animal trainer Felix Navarro, whom I reluctantly had to leave behind in Seattle.

I had only a few minutes to take in my surroundings: the blue sky full of puffy white clouds, the palm trees swaying above, the towering gray bulk of the old hotel, and, on the steps of the hotel, a phalanx of photographers, all grouped around a pretty blond woman in a pink sundress.

It was Caprice Kennedy. Her hair was so blond and so teased it looked like cotton candy. Her nails and her lipstick matched the exact pink of her dress. She clutched a small white and brown Papillon with pink ribbons on its fluffy ears.

Pepe had gone charging into the midst of the

photographers and now skidded to a halt right at Caprice's polished pink toenails.

"Caprice! Caprice!" He was squeaking. I had never heard him so excited.

She looked down at him and frowned. "Get that strange dog away from me!" she said, kicking at him with her sandaled foot.

Pepe's big brown eyes got even bigger.

"But, Caprice . . . ," he said. "It is I, Pepe!"

"Shoo, dog!" said one of the photographers, flapping his hands at him.

"You're my little Princess," Caprice cooed to her Papillon, holding it up to her lips and giving the dog a kiss, which incited a round of camera clicks. "Mommy won't let that ruffian get near you!"

Pepe came back to me, wobbling a little. His ears were down and his tail curled between his legs. He seemed to be in shock. I picked him up.

"Geri, she does not remember me!" he said.

He sounded so pathetic I thought my heart would break.

Chapter 2

Pepe was quiet during the photo shoot, which was unusual for my blabbermouth of a dog. He did seem to know how to handle the publicity, though. He managed to work his way into the front of every picture; I did my best to stay in the background. Unfortunately, Caprice's little Papillon did not appreciate Pepe hogging the 'imelight. At one point, she snapped at him, which made Caprice chide her.

"Be nice, Princess," she said with a little wag of her finger. It made for an adorable photo. Even more so when the paparazzi snapped photos of Pepe gazing up at Caprice with longing. I heard one of them say, "That Chihuahua has real star quality."

The little star was not so happy with our lodgings. While Rebecca swept Luis and Siren Song off to a bungalow by the pool, Pepe and I were ushered into a room on the fifth floor of the hotel at the end of a long hallway.

I thought it was rather charming, furnished with a shabby chic aesthetic that evoked the old days of Hollywood: faded gold satin draperies, a gilt-edged mirror on the wall across from the bed. But Pepe grumbled as he inspected the tiny bathroom and the contents of the small refrigerator tucked into a corner. According to him, he and Caprice had always stayed in the penthouse suite.

"Do you miss living with Caprice?" I asked, expecting an answer that would crush me.

"Oh no, *mi amiga*." he said with a straight face. "I far prefer our rather cramped and humble condo in chilly Seattle to living the life of luxury in Los Angeles."

Rebecca didn't even give us time to unpack before she herded us back into the limousine for a trip to the soundstage to check out the set. Caprice drove off in her low-slung convertible red Ferrari, saying she'd meet us at the studio.

"I remember that car well," said Pepe. He sounded wistful.

"Perhaps you would rather ride with Caprice," I said. I couldn't stop myself from sounding sulky. I was flashing back to my childhood and arguments with my sister about who would ride in the front passenger seat. Being the one riding beside Mom or Dad meant they loved you best.

"Not if it means being in the same car as that bitch," Pepe said. For a moment, I hoped he was talking about Caprice, but then I realized he was probably referring to Princess. "Anyway, a Hummer limo suits my style." He jumped up onto the back of the seat and curled up behind me, where he could see out the window and keep an eye on his true love, Siren Song, who was snoozing on the seat beside Rebecca.

In Seattle, if you drove down the street in a Hummer limo, most people would stop and stare. (Some of them might even throw eggs.) In L.A., no one batted an eye as our long white limousine cruised down the crowded streets.

"What is all that racket?" asked Pepe as we turned down Santa Monica Boulevard. We had made slow progress through the midafternoon traffic—sometimes it took three lights before we could proceed through an intersection.

"I don't hear anything," I told him.

"You are not a dog," he said matter-of-factly. He had made that statement more than once since we'd been together, and I sometimes wondered if he was just stating a simple fact or if he was being patronizing: like someone explaining a complicated theoretical formula, and when you say you don't understand it, they say, "Well, you're not an astrophysicist."

"I believe we are approaching the cause of the disturbance," said Pepe, craning his neck forward as our limousine slowed down. "It appears to be a protest."

"What?"

"*Sí*, a protest," Pepe continued. "Many people carrying signs and yelling and blocking our way."

The limousine had come to a complete stop as it attempted to turn right into a driveway. There was a little booth at the edge of the sidewalk and behind it a barred gate. The archway above the gate read METROLAND STUDIOS. A lot of people were marching back and forth on the sidewalk, carrying signs that read NO DOG SHOULD DANCE! and STOP CANINE SLAVERY.

"What's going on?" I asked.

"It must be that damned PETA!" said Rebecca.

"What does the Greek bread they use in making gyros have to do with any of this?" Pepe asked me.

"It's not that kind of pita," I told him.

He gave me a quizzical look.

"This is *PETA*," I explained. "People for the Ethical Treatment of Animals."

"Oh," he said. "Well that is a good thing, is it not?"

"Not in this case," I told him. "I think they might be trying to stop us from doing *Dancing with Dogs*." I turned to Rebecca. "Why are they doing this?"

"They think making dogs dance is cruel and unusual," she said.

"Why would they think that?" Pepe asked.

"I can't believe they organized this fast!" Rebecca said.

"Did you know this was going to happen?" I asked.

"Oh, we started getting threats as soon as the

Hollywood Reporter mentioned we were going to begin filming. These people are fanatics!"

The chauffeur pulled as far as he could into the driveway, and we could see the demonstrators better. Most were in their twenties. Some of the young women were almost nude and had painted their bodies to make them look like dalmatians and springer spaniels. They wore dog collars around their necks with leashes dangling down.

"I must say I like their costumes," Pepe said thoughtfully. "You should try that, Geri. I think it would be a good look for you."

"I guess my publicist is worth the money I'm spending on her," Rebecca observed.

"You arranged this?" I asked, aghast.

"Publicity is publicity." Rebecca shrugged. "Look!" She pointed out the window. I saw a TV cameraman and a reporter thrusting a microphone toward the young woman whose lithe body was painted white and covered with the black spots of a dalmatian. "We'll probably the evening news."

The chauffeur was talking to the guard in the booth, and in a few minutes, the gate slowly slid open and our limousine began to ease through it into the studio.

As we passed through the demonstrators, they shook their signs like so many leaves in a storm. The messages were weird: DOG IS GOD SPELLED BACKWARDS! and LET MY ANIMALS GO! and YOU'RE REALLY DANCING FOR DOLLARS! and PEOPLE ARE ANIMALS, TOO! and EAT TOFURKEY, SAVE A TURKEY! The strange mix of slogans made me wonder if they'd brought some signs that were left over from a previous demonstration.

"What is a Tofurkey?" Pepe asked me. "Is it better than turkey? I very much like turkey."

"I'll get you one later," I promised him.

The studio was quite impressive. There was a tall office building, which Rebecca explained was used for interior shots, like the office scenes in *Mad Men*, plus it contained the studio offices, some editing suites, and a café where we could get lunch.

"We were lucky there was a soundstage available here," Rebecca said as the chauffeur pulled up in front of the building. "Unfortunately I couldn't get the one with the in-stage pool."

"How would we have used that?" I asked.

"I thought it might provide a nice twist. We could have had the dogs perform some synchronized swimming," Rebecca said.

Pepe shuddered. He has a fear of water that he claims comes from being thrown into a swimming pool by one of Caprice's friends.

"The only problem is the tight schedule," Rebecca said. "We have to be in and out of here in a week."

"Look, there is Caprice's car!" said Pepe, checking out the parking lot. He pointed a paw at the red Ferrari parked in a handicapped spot.

"Are the other judges meeting us here?" I asked Rebecca.

"Yes, all three of them. I want to do a run-through, just to see if the setup works. That way they won't have to come back until we start filming tomorrow afternoon."

"Who are the other judges besides Caprice?"

"Oh, didn't I tell you? I've lined up animal psychic Miranda Skarbos and Nigel St. Nigel."

"Nigel St. Nigel?" That was quite a coup. Nigel St. Nigel had been the mean judge on the popular *So You Wanna Be a Star* show for four seasons. Then he disappeared. No one was sure why, although there were many rumors.

"Yes, we have to have one mean judge. Otherwise, the show won't work."

We transferred to an electric cart to get to the soundstage. Apparently they restricted the number of normal cars and trucks on the lot—I suppose the vibrations of too many heavy machines could rattle lights and wobble cameras.

As we rolled along the asphalt, down a narrow alley between the soundstages, I began to enjoy myself. The sun on my skin felt good after weeks of Seattle's gray skies and constant drizzle. Puffy white clouds floated in a sky the exact color of a sky-blue crayon. Pepe seemed happy, too, with his tongue hanging out of his mouth and his eyes closed.

The soundstages resembled the hangars where Boeing builds its jets in Seattle. They were made of corrugated steel, painted dull beige, and punctuated by red doors with numbers on them. We didn't see any other people, just empty carts parked outside the doors. One could imagine all the fantastic worlds going on inside. I would have to Google MetroLand and find out what shows were currently being filmed here.

Our soundstage was #13. I thought the number was ominous, but Rebecca didn't seem fazed.

She tried the knob and it turned. "I guess one of the judges must have gotten here before us," she said.

The inside was cavernous. The ceiling towered overhead, laced with grids of metal and dripping with cables and ropes. The walls were painted black, which gave the impression that we were standing in infinite space. A little light came in through the open door, illuminating a swath of concrete floor that was cluttered with snaking cables, but beyond that was only a dense velvety blackness. A few exit lights glowed green. They seemed to be miles away.

"Hello? Is anyone here?" Rebecca called out. Her voice died away. She sighed, exasperated. "Where are the lights?" She fumbled around on the wall for a switch.

Suddenly a light flickered in the darkness. Ahead of us, like an apparition, a stage appeared. The floor was a dull black, but it was surrounded by a luminous, white plastic border that cast an eerie glow in the dark space. A flight of glittery stairs, lit from underneath, led down to the dance floor between two bright red fluorescent fire hydrants.

"Oh, it's just as I pictured it!" said Rebecca with a little gasp of admiration. "Our set designer did a great job."

"I think the fire hydrants are a mistake," said

Pepe. "A dog is a creature of instinct, and when I see a fire hydrant, it is not dancing that comes to mind."

Rebecca hurried toward the stage, with me and Siren Song and Pepe following close behind. As we got closer, I could see that there were bleachers for the audience members rising up on either side of the stage and a sort of booth in front of the stage for the judges. A man sat in one of the judges' chairs, gazing out at the stage.

"Nigel? Is that you?" Rebecca asked. He did not respond. But then no one really expected that of him. He was known for his long silences during which the contestants would squirm.

"Wait, Geri!" said Pepe, coming to an abrupt halt. "Something is wrong! Do not go any closer."

Rebecca reached his side and put out a hand to tap Nigel on the shoulder.

"I'm so honored to be working with you, Nigel," she said.

And then she began screaming. Ignoring Pepe's frantic attempts to stop me, I ran forward, just as Nigel St. Nigel toppled sideways and fell into a pool of blood on the floor.

Chapter 3

Pepe and I knew what to do. We'd been at a crime scene before. I grabbed Pepe, who was sniffing around the corpse. I didn't want him to get any blood on his paws—then the police might want to hold him as evidence.

After calling 911, we went outside with Rebecca, who, after that one shriek, was remarkably calm. She was on the phone within minutes, first to her publicist (looking for a way to spin the death), then to the casting director (looking for a replacement for Nigel), and finally to the studio execs (trying to figure out if she could move the show to another soundstage).

Pepe was annoyed. He kept telling me he wanted to get back inside to investigate. He fancies himself a PI, and sometimes I encourage him in this belief. It makes him happy, and don't we all want our dogs to be happy?

The truth was that I was merely working for a PI named Jimmy G while I waited for the real estate market to improve so I could go back to my old job: staging houses for sale. When Jimmy G hired me, he told me I would be a junior investigator, but it turns out you need to have four hours of training and pass a test to be a PI in Washington State. So I had settled for the title of Girl Friday and would begin the training when I got back to Seattle. Meanwhile I'd brought along my copy of *Private Investigating for Dummies*, hoping to have some time to study.

I heard sirens far off in the distance. An emergency vehicle showed up first, lumbering along the narrow road between the soundstages. As it came to a stop in front of us, we saw people emerging from the buildings all over the lot. Most were guys who were dressed in jeans and T-shirts, but I also saw people in blue surgical scrubs and white lab coats clustered in front of one soundstage, and another group dressed in the clothes of the fifties outside another. I thought I recognized some of my favorite actors from *Mad Men*: the curvy redhead and Don Draper himself, in a shiny gray suit.

Of course, all the productions would have to stop as the traffic of death rolled by. The people gathered in knots, smoking and talking, but stayed at a respectful distance as the EMTs rushed through the door of the soundstage.

A few minutes later, a short, slender young man in a pair of lime-green trousers and a Hawaiian shirt came bustling up. His bleached-blond hair stuck up all over his head like a porcupine's quills and he wore horn-rimmed glasses. He juggled a drink tray bearing two tall paper coffee cups.

"What's going on here?" he asked, staring at the red and white emergency vehicle.

"Don't go in there!" I warned, but it was too late. He dashed into the soundstage. A moment later we heard his strangled cry: "No! No! No!"

He staggered back outside, his face pasty, the coffee missing. "Oh my God! Oh my God! Oh my God!" he said as he slumped against the wall of the soundstage.

"Who are you?" Rebecca snapped.

"Rodney Klamp. I'm Nigel's PA," he said, bristling with importance.

"PA as in *public announcement*?" I turned to Pepe, puzzled by the acronym.

"No, as in *personal assistant*," said Pepe. "It is a common term in Beverly Hills. Like you."

"Like me?"

"*Sí!* You are my PA." He seemed mighty proud of himself. "Ask him where he has been."

"Where have you been?" I asked.

"Isn't it obvious?" Rodney replied. "Nigel sent me out for a couple of lattes. Oh, this is all my fault!"

"Ask him why it is his fault!" Pepe told me.

"Why is it your fault?"

"Because the coffee was the wrong temperature. I told the barista one hundred eighty degrees, but by the time I got back to the soundstage, the coffee was too cold. So Nigel sent me

back. But I shouldn't have left him alone!"
Rodney wailed. "It seemed so safe. There was no
one else here. But I knew better."

"What do you mean?" I asked.

But just then the police arrived. First one
black-and-white car with two guys in the
standard dark-blue LAPD uniforms, then a
gray sedan from which emerged a pair of
plainclothes homicide detectives, one man
and one woman. They both looked like movie
stars. The woman was blond and had a long
ponytail. She wore a pretty pink jacket over a
yellow linen dress. She resembled Kyra Sedgwick from the TV show *The Closer*. The man
was a Nordic type: fair hair, strong jaw, blue
eyes. He looked a little like the vampire Eric
from *True Blood*.

"Does everybody in Hollywood look like a
movie star?" I whispered to Pepe.

"Everybody in L.A. is a movie star!" he replied.

The coroner's van pulled up next, and a short
Asian man in a white coat got out and went
inside. Soon the alley between the soundstages
was filled with black-and-white cars and cops who
were unrolling crime scene tape.

A harried studio executive in a sports coat
showed up. Rebecca confronted him. "If we're
not going to be able to shoot tomorrow morning, we're not paying for the space," she said.

"Hey, look, it's not under my control," he
said. "We have to wait until the police clear the
scene." He rushed off to talk to the crews and

actors on the other soundstages and soon had them convinced, after some arm waving and yelling, to go back inside and get back to work.

When he returned, he approached the female detective. "I need you to move the cars. Any noise will disrupt the productions going on here, and we have several important shows being filmed. Every minute not worked is money down the drain."

"Sorry," she said, "but I can't guarantee anything. We might have to rush someone to the hospital."

"That won't be necessary." The short Asian man came out of the soundstage, peeling off his blue latex gloves. "He's dead. No hurry now."

"Do you have an estimate on time of death?" asked the female detective.

"Body's still warm. I'd say he died within the hour—maybe during the last thirty minutes or so."

"Cause of death?" she asked.

"Looks like he was shot through the heart at close range. But we'll know more when we do the autopsy." He went to his van and removed a plastic case and headed back into the building. "We've got an ID on him, but it would be great to have confirmation. Any of you here know him?"

"I certainly did," said Rodney, sniffling. "That's Nigel St. Nigel!"

"Nigel St. Nigel?" The coroner seemed properly impressed.

"Yes!" said Rodney. "The meanest man on television." He wiped at his eyes with a handkerchief, which he had removed from his pocket with a flourish. "He was proud of that title."

"Where were you when he was shot?" the woman asked.

Rodney explained again about the coffee and his concerns about leaving Nigel. "He was acting weird. Almost as if he was expecting to meet someone."

"Can you think of anybody who'd want to kill him?"

Rodney let out a sound that was somewhere between a snort and a laugh. "Who didn't want to kill him? He alienated everyone he ever met! Even his parents. That contempt was not an act. He thought everyone was a fool!"

"Even you?" she asked.

Rodney's face shut down. "Do I need a lawyer?" he asked. He looked about wildly as if he expected to see one in the wings.

There probably was someone playing a lawyer on one of the soundstages, I thought.

The tall blond policeman, who introduced himself as Sam Scott, took us back into the soundstage to conduct interviews. All of the lights had been turned on and were blazing down on the stage and the judges' box. Nigel's body was still on the ground, with crime techs buzzing around it. The uniformed police officers were conducting a search, directed by the female detective. They fanned out, peering at the floor, leaving behind little yellow number markers. A photographer followed behind, snapping pictures.

All the action stopped when Caprice appeared in the doorway. She paused a moment, framed against the bright sunlight. She was wearing a short red dress, and she had her Papillon tucked into a red patent leather bag on her shoulder. She had even changed the dog's bows to match the bag and her red high heels. The room went silent. I swear the police photographer snapped a photo of her—was probably going to make a little extra money on the side selling it to the *Star*.

"What's going on here?" Caprice asked, strolling down the aisle.

"I'm sorry, Miss Kennedy," said Scott, rushing away from us and over to her. "You shouldn't be here! This is a crime scene!"

"What happened?"

"Someone was murdered."

"Who?" Her pretty face crinkled up.

"Nigel St. Nigel."

"Serves him right!" she said. "He was mean to me!" She gave the body a passing glance.

"He was mean to everyone, darling. Don't take it personally," said Rodney, stepping forward.

"Did you just arrive?" Scott asked Caprice.

"Yes," she said with a pretty pout.

I frowned. Pepe had identified her car in the parking lot earlier. Perhaps he had been wrong.

"Where's the other judge?" I asked.

Rebecca looked around. "That's a good question. Miranda was supposed to meet us here, too. I hope nothing happened to her. Otherwise, I'm down two judges." She picked up her phone and started dialing.

"If you don't mind me asking, Miss Kennedy, where have you been during the last hour or so?"

"Me?" she said. "I went to the commissary and had a chocolate mocha and a biscotti."

"At the commissary," said Scott. He pointed at Rodney, asking, "Did you notice that man there?"

"No," she said, giving Rodney a brief glance. "Can't say I did. Who is he?"

"I'm Rodney Klamp," he said. "And I can't say I saw you there, either."

"I'm hard to miss," said Caprice.

"No," Pepe mumbled, then said something that sounded like, "She is easy to miss."

"What?" I asked him.

All of a sudden, Pepe's ears perked up and he turned his head sharply toward the backstage area. "I hear something!" he exclaimed.

"I don't hear anything," I said.

I half expected him to give me his old "I am a dog" line, but instead he said, "I will investigate!" and tore off backstage.

"Pepe!" I shouted.

"What's with that dog? Where's he going?" asked Scott.

"I think he hears something," I said, starting to go after him.

"I don't hear anything," said Scott.

"You're not a dog," I called back to him.

"Hold up!" yelled Scott. "You can't take off like this! I'm going with you."

We dashed up the stairs at the back of the dance floor and found ourselves in a large room with benches around the walls. A camera was positioned in one corner. There was an open door on the other end that led out into a long room lined with makeup tables. Pepe was already at the end of the line and had turned the corner. I followed him into a welter of equipment: ladders, open and closed; coils of cable on the floor; racks full of costumes. It was dark and hard to see. I picked my way through the thicket of equipment. I could hear Scott behind me. Ahead of me, just a flicker of white in the gloom, was Pepe, scratching at a door. There was a crack of light running along the edge of it. As I got closer, I could see it was a heavy door, made of metal, and it opened inward. Pepe couldn't budge it, though he was trying with all his might.

"What is it, Pepe?" I asked.

"Through here!" he said, panting a little from the effort he was making. "The murderer left through this door!"

"Hey! Come back here!" That was Scott behind me. "Stop! I order you to stop!"

I found the handle of the door and tugged on it. Pepe darted through the opening as soon as it was wide enough for him, but it took all of my strength to get it open far enough for me to get through. The light outside was blinding after the darkness of the soundstage, and it took me a few seconds to realize what I was seeing. Pepe was standing in front of a tall young man with wild eyes and shaggy hair who was holding a gun in his hand.

Chapter 4

"Drop the gun!" Detective Scott was right behind me. He had his pistol out and trained on the assailant within a second. "I said drop the gun!"

The guy seemed confused by this simple command. He looked down at the gun in his hand, looked up at Scott, and then extended the gun.

I shuddered and turned, sure that Scott would simply blow him away.

Instead he shouted, "This is your last chance! Drop it!"

The guy froze. He glanced from side to side. Then he opened his fingers and the gun clattered to the ground.

Scott was on him in a flash and pinned him up against the side of the building. With one hand, he pulled a cell phone out of his jacket pocket and yelled into it. "Officer needs assistance! Got a suspect in back of the soundstage!"

"Hey!" The guy struggled. I wondered if I should help Scott. "You're hurting me!"

"He is not the perpetrator," said Pepe.

"What?"

"He is not the perpetrator," Pepe repeated.

"How do you know?"

"It is the smell," Pepe said. "He does not have the scent of violence."

The suspect was still struggling. "Hey, man, what are you doing?" He was dressed in jeans and a T-shirt with a logo on it.

"Put your hands behind your back!" Scott slammed him against the wall for emphasis.

"Hey, man, I didn't do anything!" the guy protested. He looked at me, his eyes pleading. "You're witnessing this, right? Police brutality!"

"You threatened him with a gun!" I said.

"I found it on the ground!" the guy said.

"Right!" That was Scott, in a grim voice, as he fitted the handcuffs around the guy's wrists, first one and then the other. *Click. Click.*

"He did find it on the ground," Pepe said, going over and sniffing at the gun.

"Get your dog away from there!" Scott ordered. "That's evidence!"

"He thinks I do not know what is evidence?" Pepe was offended. "The gun smells of the murderer and the asphalt. This man had just picked it up."

"Backup! I need backup!" That was Scott on the phone again.

"What if what he says is true?" I asked. "What if the real murderer dropped it and this guy just picked it up?"

"What if every kid from the Midwest who moved to L.A. became a star?" asked Scott with a snarl in his voice.

"I'm serious," I said.

"So am I," said Scott.

"If he killed Nigel St. Nigel, he will have gunpowder residue and possibly some blowback from the shot at close range," said Pepe, who watched a lot of *CSI* shows on TV.

"That's right," I said. "If he killed Nigel St. Nigel, you'll find gunpowder residue and some blowback."

"I don't need your help to do my job," Scott said. He was grunting with the effort of holding the man, who was still protesting, against the wall.

Pepe was sniffing the ground in widening circles. Suddenly he darted around the corner.

"Pepe! Come back!" I started to go after him.

"Hey!" Scott's attention was diverted by my attempted departure. His prisoner took advantage of that to move away from the wall. Scott grabbed him by the elbow and slammed him back against the wall.

"Ow!"

I saw blood running out of the man's mouth. At that moment, two other police officers in blue uniforms pushed their way through the door. In a second, they were all on top of the suspect, pounding on his head.

"Hey! He didn't do anything!" I said.

"Stop resisting arrest!" shouted one of the officers.

"He's not resisting arrest!"

Suddenly they turned their attention to me. "Put your hands behind your back!"

"What? I didn't do anything!"

"Turn around and put your hands behind your back!"

In a matter of minutes, they had me in handcuffs and began patting me down. Pepe came running back and tried to rescue me by biting at their ankles, but I told him to stop and he did.

"We can't both go to jail!" I told him.

"So true, Geri," he said. "One of us must be on the outside to investigate."

Luckily, Rebecca showed up on the scene, and within a few minutes, she got it all sorted out. The police released me, and we all managed to get back to the hotel in time to watch the news.

Dancing with Dogs was all over it. First the news about Nigel's murder, which ended with the announcement that a suspect was in custody: Ted Messenger, the head of a group of animal activists. That was followed by coverage of the protests outside the gate to the studio lot, with the camera lingering on the shapely young women dressed as dogs. Caprice came in a poor third, with the shots of her and Princess outside the hotel.

Rebecca was elated and ordered a magnum of champagne to be delivered to her bungalow. But I didn't want to celebrate. The events of the day had worn me out, and I just wanted to have a glass of Chardonnay before going to bed. I headed for the hotel bar with Pepe. Apparently it is fine to bring your dog to the bar at the Chateau Marmont. Stranger things were seen there, like the woman wearing a shimmery short dress made of beer can tabs and a guy with long gray hair in a ponytail, wearing a tartan kilt. Pepe ran up and down the bar, deftly dodging through glasses and plates.

"Nice to see a Chihuahua in here," the bartender said. "We used to get a lot of them, but now the designer dogs are all the rage."

"Yeah!" said the guy in the kilt who was sitting next to me. "Labradoodles. And Golden Doodles. Chorkies. And Pomerhuahuas."

"I wouldn't mind making some Pomerhuahuas," said Pepe, who was obviously thinking of his Pomeranian sweetheart.

Pepe was a big hit at the bar. The patrons plied him with nibbles of their happy hour hors d'oeuvres (which he enjoyed) and their cocktails and draft beers (which he spurned).

I, on the other hand, was enjoying my glass of Chardonnay when I felt a hand on my back. I turned around and there was the guy I had last seen in handcuffs. He looked much the worse for wear. One eye was puffed up and almost closed. His lip was also puffed up. His T-shirt, which read PETA, was splattered with dried blood from the cops' beating on him. Despite that, I thought he was somewhat attractive.

"What are you doing here?" I asked.

"I need to talk to you," he said, sitting down on the stool next to me. He held out his hand. "I'm Ted Messenger."

"Oh!" I said. "I thought you were in jail."

"Posted bond. We've got a great lawyer on retainer."

"Why do you want to talk to me?"

"You're the only person who believed me when I said I had just found the gun."

"It wasn't me," I said. "My dog told me that."

"Really?"

"Yes, really."

"You talk to your dog?"

"Yes."

"And he talks back?"

"Yes."

"OK."

"What do you mean OK? No one believes me when I say my dog talks."

"I do!"

"Really?" I took another look at him. He seemed to be sincere. His big brown eyes were almost as ernest as Pepe's.

"Of course. Dogs are sentient beings. We know that. So it makes sense they would be able to communicate with us. It's just that most people don't have the ability to listen to them."

"That is so true, amigo," said Pepe, who had noticed my new companion and come sauntering down the bar.

"Can you hear him?" I asked Ted, hopeful.

"What?"

"He just spoke. Did you hear that?"

Ted shook his head. "I don't have your abilities," he said with a shrug. He must have noticed my disappointment. "Have you always been able to communicate with animals?"

"Oh no," I said. "Just this dog. He's special." I

patted Pepe on the top of his velvety little head. "We've been working together ever since I got him," I said. I dug around in my pocket and pulled out one of the cards I had made for me and Pepe. It read SULLIVAN AND SULLIVAN, INVESTIGATORS. "Here's one of our cards."

Ted examined it. "You're a private investigator?"

"Sort of," I said. "I'm a PI in training."

"Good enough," he said. "I'll pass this along to my lawyer. He's probably going to want to talk to you to establish my alibi."

"What were you doing there anyway?" I asked.

"Well, I was trying to figure out how to sneak onto the lot. And I got my chance when the police arrived. We were told to leave, but no one was watching the gate. So I slipped in and was looking for a back door to Soundstage Thirteen. I needed to figure out how to get access during the show."

"What were you going to do if you got on the soundstage?" I asked.

"We go undercover and film," he said. "We're trying to document cases of animal abuse."

"What makes you think the producers would harm dogs?" I asked.

"People will do a lot of crazy things for entertainment. Have you ever watched those shows where people have to face their fears, like stand in a room full of tarantulas, or those shows where the contestants get knocked into the water or mud while competing for prizes?"

"No, I don't watch those," I said. "I don't enjoy watching people get hurt."

"You should, Geri," said Pepe. "It is *muy chistoso* to see the stupid tricks that people will do for money."

"Well, since reality TV shows often pander to the lowest common denominator," said Ted, "we figured they might exploit the dogs. You know, make them do dangerous stunts, just to get laughs. We want to make sure that doesn't happen."

"Well, that sounds like a noble purpose," I said. "If I can help, just let me know."

"That may happen sooner than you think," Ted said with a wink.

Chapter 5

Bright and early the next morning, Pepe and I headed out for our first rehearsal with mixed feelings. The mix was divided like this: Pepe was supremely confident, and I was supremely anxious.

A town car picked us up at the hotel and dropped us off in front of an old two-story building. The sign above the door read ACME BUILDING. Glass doors opened into a lobby. A colored piece of paper on the wall marked with an arrow indicated we should go upstairs for the *Dancing with Dogs* rehearsal.

A flight of linoleum-covered stairs led up to the second floor. Pepe amazed me by taking the stairs with seemingly no effort. Each of the stairs was almost as tall as he was—they'd be about six feet tall if they were increased proportionately to my own height. How he did it, especially this early in the morning, was beyond me.

"There you are!" It was Rebecca, dressed in a pair of black yoga pants and a black tank top, standing in a doorway just down the hall to our left. "You're the last to arrive." She consulted her clipboard. "I've assigned you to room two-oh-nine." She pointed at the last door on the left side of the hall.

It was an old building with creaky wooden floors. The doors had glass windows. As we went down the hall, I could look through them and see all the rooms were occupied. I caught glimpses of some of the other contestants on the show: a svelte young man with a silky Yorkie; a gray-haired woman with a border collie; a punky-looking young woman with a black standard poodle, perfectly groomed, complete with the pom-poms around his paws. We passed through successive waves of music: a rap song, something with a Latin beat, and a waltz. Pepe was busy sniffing along the bottom of every door.

"You will be sorry!" he said to each unseen opponent. "You can never prepare sufficiently to defeat Pepe el Macho." Halfway down the hall, his demeanor changed. "Ah, Siren Song! *¡Mi amor!* You smell as sweet as roast beef."

"What?" It was hard to imagine roast beef as a seductive scent. Perhaps to a dog.

I peered in the window and saw Rebecca's little Pomeranian, Siren Song, dancing with a good-looking Hispanic man. It was Luis Montoya, formerly Rebecca's gardener and currently her bodyguard. Or perhaps personal assistant. I wasn't sure which.

"Why is Luis dancing with Siren Song?" I asked Rebecca.

"Well, I can't dance with her!" Rebecca said. "Why do you think I brought him along?"

Actually, I could think of many reasons to bring Luis along, but I didn't want to admit them.

"You are blushing, Geri," Pepe pointed out.

"Shut up!" I said.

Rebecca looked miffed.

"Not you!" I said. "I was talking to Pepe."

"He *is* making a lot of noise!" Rebecca said.

Actually he was warbling a serenade to Siren Song. It was in Spanish, but I recognized a few words: *mi amor* and *corazon*. It seemed to be having an effect on Siren Song. She had been prancing around on her back feet, turning in circles, but as Pepe caroled his words of love, she began faltering and looking toward the door.

"Come away, Pepe," I said. "We have to dance!"

"We'll only be here for a few hours. We start filming at the soundstage right after lunch. Everybody needs to be up to speed." Rebecca paused and glanced at her wristwatch.

"So the police are finished with the crime scene?"

"They promised me they'd be done by one p.m."

"And you got another judge?"

"Oh yes, didn't I tell you? Beverly Holywell."

"The English dog whisperer?" She was a legend in the field of animal training. Even before I adopted Pepe, I had watched some of her videos. It was miraculous, the way she soothed vicious animals and calmed neurotic ones with just a soft tone of voice and a sensible attitude.

"What about Miranda Skarbos?" I asked. "Did you ever find her?"

Rebecca frowned. "She claimed that her dog warned her not to go to the set. Said something bad was going to happen."

"Sound like she really is psychic," I said.

"It sounds like her dog is the one that is psychic," said Pepe.

Rebecca made a tsking sound. "I can't believe you'd fall for that sort of nonsense, Geri. It's all made up! They always have someone on the inside feeding them information."

"Well, if her inside source knew Nigel was going to be murdered, then that's someone the police should interview," I said.

We had reached the last door. "Here you go! One of our choreographers couldn't make it, but this guy showed up at the hotel this morning, and he seems to be qualified. I let him pick out the music. And by the way"—she checked her clipboard again—"your dance is the fox-trot."

Rebecca pulled open the door and practically pushed me and Pepe inside, then abruptly closed the door and left. A soft swing song was playing on an iPod set in a dock on the broad windowsill. Gray light filtered into the room through cloudy windows and lit up the scuffed wood floor and rippled off the bank of mirrors that lined one wall.

A tall man stood in front of the mirrors, pacing back and forth in smooth, gliding steps. He had slicked-back dark hair and a muscled body that was well displayed in his tight bright orange polyester T-shirt and sprayed-on black jeans. It took me a minute to realize it was the PETA guy, Ted, whom I'd talked to at the hotel bar last night.

"You!" I said. "You sure get around! What are you doing here?"

He glided over and held out his hand. "Shhh! You'll blow my cover!"

"What cover?"

"I'm Eduardo Galliano, dance instructor, but you can call me Ed."

"I'm not going to call you Ed."

"You can call me irritated," said Pepe. "Geri, you must tell Rebecca!"

"You've got to help me!" he said, grabbing my hands.

"But he'll ruin our chances of winning the competition," Pepe said. "I must win to impress Siren Song."

"But you'll ruin our chances—" I began, and then stopped. Actually, that would be fine with me. Pepe might be disappointed if we got eliminated from the show early, but I wouldn't. There were so many things I wanted to see in L.A.: the Los Angeles County Museum of Art, the Getty, the Museum of Jurassic Technology, Venice Beach. Maybe I'd even take Pepe back to his old haunts on Rodeo Drive and see if any of the shopkeepers recognized him.

"I used to be a dance instructor for Arthur Murray," said Ed or Ted or whatever. "That's how I paid for college. If anyone can teach you to dance, I can!"

"Did you major in dance?" I asked.

"Psychology. Until I was put in charge of the monkeys in the research center—"

"Focus, Geri! Focus!" Pepe snapped. "We are wasting time!"

"I guess we should get started," I said, giving in to my dog's agenda.

"Yes." Ted's face fell. He evidently wanted to share the story of his conversion to animal activism.

"You can tell me later," I said. I wanted to reassure him. "Right now, I'm worried about learning to dance. I'm a natural-born klutz. And I've never done the fox-trot."

"It's not so hard," said Ted. "Let me show you. It's slow, slow, quick, quick." He began gliding around the floor. "Just follow me."

I tried, I really did, but I kept pausing on one foot when I was supposed to be going forward and going quick when I was supposed to be going slow. Pepe, however, seemed to be doing fine.

"Wow," he said, standing back and watching us. "Your dog has rhythm!"

"*Sí*, I can foot it as light as any fox!" said Pepe, picking up his little feet, lifting them high, and putting them down with delicate precision.

"He looks just like a fox!" said Ted in an amazed tone.

"Naturally, as I studied with the great Renard," said Pepe proudly.

"I suppose you are now going to claim you talk to foxes!" I said.

"I would never claim that," said Ted.

"Of course I do," Pepe said with pride. "Did

you think my ability to communicate across species applies only to your species, Geri?"

"I do not like your tone, mister!" I said.

"I'm sorry if I offended you," Ted said.

"I'm not talking to you. I'm talking to my dog!" I explained.

"Oh, and what's he saying?"

"He claims he learned to dance from a fox."

"I must say he's very convincing as one," Ted said, studying Pepe with a tilt of his head. "It gives me a great idea for the choreography. I was thinking of something traditional, a sort of Ginger Rogers and Fred Astaire number, but now I'm thinking, what if we take the story of Little Red Riding Hood and pair her up with a fox instead of a wolf?"

"What?"

"Yes! A story! That will help you win the competition." He plucked his iPod out of its dock and began poking buttons. In a few seconds, we heard the opening lines of "Lil' Red Riding Hood," as sung by Sam the Sham & the Pharaohs.

"I think this dude has some good ideas," said Pepe. "You can tell me what big teeth I have!" And he lifted his lips to reveal his tiny pointed teeth.

"Your dog is such a ham!" Ted said. "He's in character already. Here, let's try this!"

He put us through a series of dance movements designed to depict the rambling walk of Little Red on her way to Grandma's (I was pretty good at the rambling walk) while Pepe skulked behind me, keeping a watchful eye. Then he ran ahead of me and preened himself as I alternately approached him and backed off, surprised by his big ears (Pepe does have big ears) and big eyes (Pepe does have big eyes) and big teeth (well, not so big but they look pretty menacing when Pepe combines them with a growl).

Ted applauded as we completed the routine for the third time. "Your dog is a natural!"

"*Sí,* I have won the heart of many a senorita with my suave moves," said Pepe.

"But you still need some work!" Ted said, turning to me. "Private lesson? Later tonight?"

"I think not," said Pepe, getting in between us. "We will be busy investigating. We have to catch a murderer."

Chapter 6

After the rehearsal, we were transported in town cars to the soundstage. I'd never realized how many people were required to produce a television show. The soundstage, which had been so empty and dark and spooky the night before, was now swarming with activity. Rebecca took us around and introduced us. There were production assistants and an assistant to the producer, genny operators and crane operators and boom operators, focus-pullers and clapper-loaders, gaffers and grips.

"I know what a gaffer is," Pepe told me. "That is the hombre who gaffs the large fish and brings it aboard the boat."

"No, Pepe, that's a different kind of gaffer."

"I beg to differ," he said. "I have seen them gaff marlin on the charter boats off Cabo San Lucas many times."

"Don't tell me you worked on a fishing boat?"

"*Sí,*" he proudly stated. "I was a deckhand

on the *Coronado* for Captain Cortez, the most famous of the fishing skippers."

"How could you have been a deckhand?"

"Easy," he said. "My job was to chase off the seagulls when they landed, trying to steal our bait. I was quick, efficient, and very menacing." He bared his little teeth and growled. "Those birds never got any bait past this *perro*, I can tell you."

Rebecca also introduced us to a guy named Jake, a big redheaded man in a T-shirt and jeans who was an animal safety representative, certified by the American Humane Society. According to Rebecca, there had to be one on every set, to guarantee that the animals weren't being mistreated. I wondered if that would assuage Ted's concerns.

There was also a veterinarian, a young woman named Alice who had big blue eyes and curly blond hair. She looked far too young to be a vet. They had given her a little space of her own, in the middle of the soundstage. It was furnished with a waist-high stainless-steel table and a rolling cupboard of supplies like one might expect to see in a vet's office. She told Pepe he was a cutie and gave him a treat. He was totally smitten.

According to Rebecca, the most important person we met was Shelley, the second assistant director, a young woman dressed in a black T-shirt and black jeans who wore her dark hair in a ponytail high on the back of her head.

"Oh, you're the Chihuahua couple!" she said when Rebecca introduced us. The staff hadn't bothered to learn our names. They simply referred to us by the breed names of our dogs. It seemed the casting director had gone for diversity with one dog from many of the most popular breeds. "You're supposed to be in wardrobe right now—then you've got ten minutes for your walk-through on-set."

We were on a ruthless schedule, and it was Shelley's job to keep us on track.

"Come on in!" said Robyn, the young woman in charge of costumes, as we entered her area. She had black hair and bangs chopped off right above her penciled-in dark eyebrows.

"Red Riding Hood!" she called to her assistant, who plucked a red dress from a rack of clothes.

Robyn had come to morning rehearsals to measure us and get a head start on the costumes. After a quick consult, we decided on a red silk dress, cut on the bias, to give me a forties look. I was amazed by how quickly her staff had produced the garment. The dress fit like a dream. The skirt fluttered deliciously whenever I made the slightest move. It might even create the illusion that I could dance.

"And for Pepe, the fox costume." Robyn took a long, red foxtail off the rack. Long, puffy, and a perfect red-orange hue, it looked so real I could hardly believe it was made entirely out of feathers. "Let me put your dog on the table so I can get this fitted."

"What a good dog!" Robyn cooed as she

worked on him. "And the tail fits him like a glove."

"That is a mixed metaphor," Pepe responded.

"Actually, it was a simile," I told him.

"Simile-schimile!" he snorted.

Robyn set him on the floor. "Try wagging your tail for me, Pepe."

Pepe strutted over to the nearest mirror and studied himself, his tail twitching. "If I say so myself, I am *muy* foxy!"

"I swear," Robyn said, watching him, "I've seen all the dogs, and yours has the most personality. My money is on you two to win!"

After our costume fitting, we headed to the main stage for our walk-through. Lighting technicians were making last-minute adjustments to some of the huge lights above the stage, and cameramen fiddled with the three big cameras that would film our show.

The set was, as Pepe said, "*magnifico*!" The dance floor was shaped like a giant hexagon and covered with black rubber, to make it easy for the dogs' nails to grip. We stood at the top of a set of stairs designed for grand entrances onto the dance floor.

"Don't worry, Geri," Ted said, coming up behind me. "You'll be fine!"

Was it that obvious I was worried? And why wasn't he? Security was high because of the protestors, and we all had to show our IDs at the gate. I wondered how Ted had gotten through security. Maybe he had a fake ID.

"Let's walk through the routine before we do it to music," Ted said. We headed down the stairs.

"Oh, look, there's Jake!" I said, spotting the animal safety representative sitting in the front row of the audience. "He must be watching to make sure the dogs aren't being asked to do anything that would be dangerous."

Ted whirled around and faced the back of the room, his head down. "Damn!" he said. "He can't see me."

"Why not?"

"He knows who I really am," Ted muttered. "We were in a documentary, debating about the welfare of animals in the entertainment industry."

"Surely you're on the same side!" I said. "You both want to protect animals."

"We do, but they don't!" Ted said with contempt. "They're just shills of the entertainment industry. They get paid to do this job by the very people they are supposed to be monitoring. That's why I'm here. To make sure the job is done right."

"So what does this mean?" I asked.

"It means you're going to have to walk through the routine without me," Ted said. "I'm sorry. Maybe I can arrange to have him distracted." He headed back up the stairs, his head still down.

I looked at Pepe.

"Do not fret! I will coach you, Geri!" he said. And it was true; he knew the whole routine. We signaled the sound guy to turn on our music and went through the routine. Pepe slinked and I rambled, he did arabesques and I did pirouettes, and we even managed a few paws *de chassez.* Close to the end of the routine, someone came over and tapped Jake on the shoulder. He got up and hurried away. Then Ted appeared. He had apparently been watching from the back of the bleachers.

"You did great!" he said, strolling down to the stage. "Let's just review the last part."

"How did you get rid of Jake?" I asked.

"Got someone to tell him there was a dogfight backstage. That got him going."

Ted walked us through the last bars of the routine, counting out the beats, until he came up with something he liked. Then we left the stage on our way to hair and makeup. As we made our way through the confusing warren of rooms backstage, Pepe suddenly stopped. "Say, is that not Senor Rodney over there? The personal assistant to *el muerto,* Nigel St. Nigel?"

I spotted the guy he was talking about. Sure enough, it was Rodney. I would have recognized his spiky bleached-blond hair anywhere. "Yes, it is," I said. "I wonder what he's doing here."

"I think he is gophering again," said Pepe.

"*Gophering?*"

"*Sí.* That is what personal assistants do, no?"

Rodney spotted us and came hurrying over.

"*Hola,* Senor Rodney," said Pepe.

"What are you doing here?" I asked.

"I've got a new gig." He grinned. "I'm the assistant to the assistant to the assistant director!"

"That is some title," said Pepe. "I do not wish to boast, Geri," he told me. "But I began one rung higher when I started out with Captain Cortez. I was the assistant to the assistant deckhand. I was in line to become bosun's mate by the time I left the ship."

I gave my dog a dirty look, then realized that Rodney hadn't heard his crass remark. (When you've got a talking dog, it's often easy to forget that nobody else can understand him.)

"Congratulations, I guess!" I said.

"Oh yes, it's definitely a good thing," he said. "I'm trying to learn everything I can about the film business. Rebecca agreed to take me under her wing. Meanwhile, I'm helping out here. One of the assistants didn't show up today."

That made the second person who hadn't shown up today. I wondered if I should be worried.

"Speaking of which, do you know where I could find the Yorkie? She's dancing after the border collie."

"No," I said. We were not supposed to see each other's numbers until the performance— I guess they thought we might steal moves.

"Yorkie, hmmm?" Pepe mused. "I do not know that breed. What type of *perro* is she? Large, small, shapely, and scent-full?"

"I thought your heart belonged to Siren Song," I told my would-be Lothario.

"*Sí*, it does," he answered. "But I still have eyes and a nose, do I not?"

"Oh, Siren Song," said Rodney, glancing at his clipboard. "She doesn't go on until later. Excuse me, but I've got to go find the Yorkie." With that, Rodney hurried away before I could ask him for directions.

But Pepe seemed to know right where to find the makeup station, a row of chairs facing a row of mirrors lined up against a back wall of the soundstage. How did he do it? I did not ask. He would only have told me that I was not a dog.

Next to the makeup area was a grooming station for the dogs, complete with a stainless-steel sink with a nozzle and one of those stainless-steel tables with a hanging collar that fit over the dog's neck to hold the animal still while the groomer used the sharp clippers.

Pepe shivered, looking at the setup. "I do not need a bath," he said. His tail was between his legs. Robyn had taken off the foxtail. We would put the costumes back on after our dinner.

"You could use a bath," I said. "You smell like a dog. And your toes smell like corn chips."

"If that is so," said Pepe, "I do not know why you would want to eradicate such a pleasant aroma."

The groomer came over. He was a slight young black man, with long dreads that hung down his back. "I'll take your little Chihuahua," he said, bending down to pick up Pepe.

"I am not a little dog," said Pepe.

"He's not really a little dog," I said.

"That's what they all think," said the guy, who introduced himself as Reynaldo.

Then I realized who he was. He had won the reality TV show that pitted dog groomers against each other to determine who was the best groomer in the country.

"Hey! I watched your show!" I said. "You were great!" He had been the groomer who had the best rapport with the dogs. "You're in good hands, Pepe," I said as Reynaldo whisked him away and plunged him into a plastic tub of soapy water.

While Pepe was undergoing this torment, I was led over to a chair in front of a mirror, which was torment for me. I never think I look good enough. My hair is too frizzy. My face too round. My lips too large.

My stylist, Zack, a young man with a shaved head and fully tattooed arms, fluffed up my hair with his fingers and told me what he was going to do. "First a shampoo, then I'll blow-dry your hair and use a little product to—"

"Just make me beautiful," I said, and closed my eyes and surrendered. To my surprise, he did. When I opened my eyes fifteen minutes later, I saw this pinup girl from the forties staring back at me. She had arched eyebrows, bright red pouty lips, and a smooth brunette pageboy with two gorgeous spit curls at the temples.

"Wow!" I said. But I was even more impressed by Pepe's transformation. Apparently after the bath, they had airbrushed his back and the top of his head with a reddish brown dye, leaving his underbelly white. I hardly recognized my dog.

"*Dios mio,* Geri, you are *linda! ¡Muy linda!*" Pepe told me. Then he appraised his own appearance in the full-length mirror. "As for myself, the reddish tone is *bueno,* but the white belly makes me look like the two-tone loafers, Jimmy G, is so fond of. But I hope you know I am no kind of loafer! I will dance my tail off!"

We didn't have time to go to the commissary, so we browsed the craft service table that was over by the back door. I got a yogurt and a banana; Pepe was pleased when they offered him some sliced ham and cheese from the sandwiches. We ate outside, sitting on folding chairs. The sun was shining, but there was a cool breeze blowing. Still it was fun to watch people walk by and try to guess what show they were working on.

We thought we saw a group of actors from the TV show *Criminal Minds.* Pepe was most impressed. He said that the FBI profilers would have solved Nigel St. Nigel's murder before lunch, but alas, we didn't have their kind of budget.

Then it was back to the costume area with Robyn putting the final touches on our costumes when Rodney came bustling in carrying a large package: a small cardboard box wrapped in layers of duct tape.

"Delivery for you!" Rodney said.

"For me?"

"Actually it's for a Jimmy Gerrard," Rodney said, holding it out so I could read the address. It read JIMMY GERRARD AGENCY, CARE OF GERI SULLIVAN.

That was weird. "That's the agency I work for in Seattle," I said.

"Why would Jimmy G be getting a package here?" Pepe asked.

"I don't know," I told him.

"You two need to be onstage in ten minutes," said Rodney. "The German shepherd is almost done with his routine. Are you ready?"

"I'm as ready as I'll ever be," I said.

Pepe was more enthusiastic with his "*¡Claro que sí!*" Too bad no one could hear him but me.

I took the package from Rodney. I expected it to be heavy, but it was surprisingly light. I shook it and something rattled inside. Whatever it was, I hoped it hadn't been broken. I took it with me, not knowing what else to do with it for the moment.

Chapter 7

Rodney parked us in the greenroom, which was near the stage. They called it the greenroom, but it was really a space that had been soundproofed, and the walls were a pale blue-green. Apparently this allowed them to project any background they wanted behind us. It was set up with lights, a mike, and a stationary camera so they could do interviews of us talking about the show.

"I wonder what it is?" I said, setting down the package.

"I will let you know," said Pepe, "as soon as I get a good sniff."

"Do you really think you can tell just from smelling it?"

"You doubt my keen olfactory abilities?" He looked up at me, wrinkling his nose, for emphasis I guess, as he continued. "A dog's nose is a hundred thousand times more sensitive than a human's." There it is again. That sense of canine superiority. Do all dogs have it, or only Chihuahuas?

"Go for it!" I said.

Pepe sniffed high. He sniffed low, snorting a bit as he went. Finally, his little brown nose stopped quivering, and he stepped back from the package. "I cannot yet tell you what is inside, but I can tell you one thing with absolute certainty."

"What's that?"

"Whoever handled this last was eating Nacho Cheese Doritos."

"What? Are you sure?"

"*Sí*. It is not Cool Ranch or Salsa Verde or any of the rest, but most definitely *Nacho Cheese*. I would bet my last can of dog food on it."

"OK, I guess I'll take your word for it," I said, forever surprised by my tiny pooch's talents. "Maybe the guy who delivered it was eating Doritos."

"No," Pepe said emphatically. "The nacho cheese smell emanates from beneath the plastic wrap and duct tape—therefore it is the object inside the package that carries the telltale odor. The outside smells only of Natural American Spirit tobacco, meaning the deliveryman was a smoker."

"Oh," I said.

"*Oh*?" he said sarcastically. "That is all you have to say, Geri? This is our first clue. It may be *muy importante*!"

"A clue to what?" I asked. "The snack habits of whoever sent this?"

"Well!" he huffed. "It is better than nothing, is it not?"

"I guess so."

"Mark my words," he told me. "Whoever sent this had orange stains on their fingers."

"Fine. Fine. Whatever you say." I was nervous about the performance. I hate waiting. "I guess I'll call Jimmy G and let him know about it." I pulled out my cell phone and dialed Jimmy G's number. To my surprise, he answered.

"What's up, doll?" he asked.

I told him about the mysterious package.

"Nothing to identify who sent it?"

"Just that whoever it was likes Nacho Cheese Doritos," I said, thinking it was funny.

But it wasn't funny to Jimmy G. "You said Nacho Cheese? Not Cool Ranch? Or Salsa Verde?"

"No, definitely Nacho Cheese."

"That's a cause for concern. Don't let that package out of your sight! Jimmy G has to get down to L.A. immediately!" And he hung up.

"That was weird," I told Pepe.

Just then Rodney came bustling in with a clipboard. "You're up next. Get out there!"

"Can you find a safe place for this package while we're dancing?" I asked.

"Sure," he said. "Just leave it here. I'll take care of it. Now get going!" He pointed us toward a gap in the black curtains that shielded the stage. I could see a blazing light through them. Beyond that . . . the audience, the judges, the dance floor. My stomach lurched.

"¡Vámanos!" said Pepe, trotting toward the

light. A wave of applause began, swelled, and crashed. We stood at the edge of the set, at the top of the stairs.

"And our next contestants, Geri Sullivan and her Chihuahua, Pepe!"

A slow spatter of applause followed. I froze.

"Geri!" Pepe circled around me. He looked so silly with his tail waving. "Geri! Just follow my lead!" And he dashed down the steps and onto the stage. A murmur of laughter from the audience. The music curled around me, the low, sexy voice of Sam the Sham coaxing Little Red Riding Hood into the woods. I tiptoed down the stairs, clutching my basket.

Blinded by the lights, I could not see the audience but imagined them as a huge beast waiting to devour me. Pepe was slinking around the edges of the stage, his eyes focused on me. The audience was laughing softly, as he was clearly scheming on how to seduce me. It helped that my role required me to act slightly confused and naïve, so I was totally in character.

We made it through the number, thanks to Pepe's cues. He had memorized the entire routine and kept feeding me the next move. "A pirouette! Now sliding steps back. Slow, slow, quick, quick. Turn! And act surprised when you see me behind you!"

At last it was over, and I lay sprawled on the stage in front of the judge's box, with Pepe on top of me, his little white fangs at my arched, bare throat. The house lights came on and the applause began. It was huge, like thunder. Pepe hopped off of me and began strolling around, bowing to the audience. They roared.

I got up slowly—my legs trembling—and took a few bows myself. It felt good. Pepe and I took bow after bow. Finally the applause died away. I heard Rebecca's voice calling me over to stand beside her on the little dais in front of the judges. Besides producing the show, Rebecca was also the MC. She wore a short red dress with a feathery skirt and super-high heels.

I picked Pepe up and clasped him in my arms. "You were *magnifico*, Geri!" he whispered in my ear.

"*Gracias, amigo!*" I whispered back.

Of the judges, the only one I recognized was Caprice. She was wearing a loosely crocheted white dress woven through with tinsel, so the lights glinted off it. Her Papillon, wearing a diamond collar, sat on her lap.

"What did you think, Caprice?" Rebecca asked.

Caprice narrowed her kohl-rimmed eyes. "The idea was cute. The dancing left a little to be desired. This dog—what's his name?"

"Pepe!" squeaked Pepe, his ears perking up.

"Pepe," I said. My voice wobbled a little.

"Pepe?" Caprice's voice was thoughtful. "I used to have a little Chihuahua named Pepe."

The Papillon in her lap started growling. She clearly remembered her previous encounter with Pepe.

"You, Princess, are nothing but a usurper," Pepe told her.

"Pepe, shush!" I said, forgetting that no one else could hear him.

Caprice tapped the Papillon on the nose. "Don't be jealous, Princess! Mommy loves you best."

"She says that to all the *perros*," Pepe told Princess.

"The Chihuahua has star quality, that's for sure," said Caprice. "I give them a seven."

"That is all?" Pepe was indignant.

"Thanks, Caprice! Let's move along. What about you, Beverly?" Rebecca turned to the next judge, a middle-aged woman wearing a brown tweedy jacket, buttoned tight across her capacious bosom. Beverly had a sagging face, with jowls and a double chin. She looked like a bulldog.

"I have to say the dog was focused on the owner, which is what we want to see." This must be the English animal trainer, judging by her accent. "And the signals were so subtle. Couldn't even spot them. Entertaining routine and excellent execution. I'd have to give this duo an eight," Beverly said.

A wild burst of applause.

Finally Rebecca turned to the third judge: a red-haired woman with a thin face, two high spots of color on her cheekbones, and a beaky nose. She favored a kind of gypsy look with long, dangling earrings, bangles up and down her skinny arms, and a purple chiffon top that exposed her prominent collarbone. This must be Miranda Skarbos, the pet psychic.

"This was extraordinary," she said, leaning forward in her eagerness. "It's almost as if the two of you were communicating telepathically. You work as one. I have to give you a ten."

An even larger burst of applause.

A huge scoreboard, like the ones found in football stadiums, lit up, just to the left of the stairway, and our names began flashing at the top of the list of contestants.

"That gives Geri and Pepe a total score of twenty-five and moves them into the lead for this round," said Rebecca. There was a sharp edge in her voice. I noticed that we had displaced Siren Song, who had previously been in first place.

Rebecca motioned for us to exit to the left of the stage, and we stumbled out. I felt light-headed. Pepe was dancing around me in circles.

"We did it, Geri! We are *numero uno!*" he said.

"I believe there's still one more team performing tonight," I said.

"Ah, they will be *nada* compared to us," said Pepe.

"Over here!" It was Shelley, with her clipboard. She waved us back into the greenroom, where we sat on a sofa.

All the contestants and their dogs were there. When Pepe got close to Siren Song, Max, the poodle, snapped at him. Pepe snapped back, saying, "Snap all you want, you prissy puffball poodle *perro!* Jealousy will get you nowhere."

I'd been a little worried when Rebecca said that Max was our biggest competition. But Pepe seemed to put him in his place. I did, however, think it odd that she didn't mention her own dog, Siren Song.

Then I remembered Jimmy G's package and looked around for it. But I couldn't find it anywhere in the greenroom. I'd have to ask Rodney where he put it.

"I do not know about you," Pepe said to me when they finally called us back to the stage for the final results. "But I, for one, am *muy contento* that Miranda Skarbos is one of the judges."

"Oh yes?"

"Of course," he said with a big, doggy smile. "As a psychic, she will already know that we will win."

"What if she doesn't?"

"Then she is no kind of psychic!"

Chapter 8

In the end, our score of twenty-five still held the top spot. The Yorkie was the one eliminated in this round.

"Yorkie-dorky!" said Pepe. "*Uno* down, *quatro* to go!"

"Pepe!" I said. "That's not acting like a gracious winner."

"Better than acting like a gracious loser," he told me.

I was looking forward to going back to my room, putting up my aching feet, and drinking a glass of wine. But Pepe insisted we rent a car and set off to investigate.

"Investigate what?" I asked.

"We must find the murderer, as we did in our first case," Pepe said.

"We didn't really find the murderer," I pointed out. "The murderer found us!"

Pepe ignored me. "What does it say in your book about private investigating?"

"It says that private investigators should leave investigations of homicide to the police!"

Pepe ignored me. "Motive, means, and opportunity. That is the key to solving a murder. We know the means: the gun. We know there was an opportunity because Senor Rodney left Senor St. Nigel alone when he went out for coffee. But we do not know the motive."

"Yes, what motive could anyone have for killing the meanest man in the world?"

As usual, Pepe did not recognize my sarcasm. It is one of his few failings.

"*Sí*, that is what we must investigate," he said. "That is why we are heading to Nigel St. Nigel's hacienda."

The concierge at the hotel had arranged the car rental, and Pepe insisted on a low-slung red BMW convertible, which he declared was just the right size for him. Since Rebecca was footing the bill, I went along with Pepe's request.

I did feel I belonged in California as we drove down Sunset Boulevard. The wind blew through my curls and ruffled the tips of Pepe's long ears. The sky was an unnaturally cheerful shade of blue; the street was framed by palm trees. It wound and curved past palatial estates and manicured lawns and low hedges. Every few blocks, a distinctive brown triangular sign reminded us that we were in Beverly Hills.

"How are we going to find Nigel's hacienda?" I asked Pepe. "Are you going to sniff it out?"

"You would be surprised," Pepe said, "but, no,

my dear Sullivan, I have another plan. All we need is a map to the homes of the stars. And we should see a vendor any moment!"

"What?"

"Right there!" He was standing on his hind legs, with his front legs pressed against the door so he could see over the edge.

Sure enough, at the side of the road was a guy wearing a funny rainbow umbrella on his head, with a big homemade sign that read STAR MAPS $10. He came running up as soon as I pulled over, and within a few minutes, I was inspecting a color photocopy of a map with stars marking various addresses on the curving streets of Beverly Hills. I finally found a star marking the location of Nigel's house, which was apparently just outside of Beverly Hills on a residential street a few blocks off Benedict Canyon.

The property, which covered about the equivalent of a Seattle city block, was completely surrounded by an eight-foot-tall box hedge, perfectly trimmed in a rectangular shape. The only entry was via a concrete paved driveway, blocked by a black metal gate. Behind the gate, the driveway curved away and disappeared behind a bank of hedges and shapely shrubs, so we couldn't see the house, just the steep slate roofs and towers that loomed above the hedge. It looked a bit like a French château.

"What now?" I asked Pepe, pulling over and parking on the quiet side street. There were no sidewalks. No wonder no one ever walks in L.A.

"We must find a way to make an entry," said Pepe. "Let us go check it out!"

He hopped up onto the back of the car and then down onto the narrow strip of grass between the street and the hedge.

"Pepe, I don't think this is a good idea," I said, getting out of the car and looking around. The other houses were also hidden behind hedges and fences and trees. There was no one around. Just the shush of traffic down on Sunset Boulevard.

Pepe was sniffing along the hedge. "*¡Muy interesante!*" he said. And then a few minutes later, "This might be important."

"What is it?" I asked, trailing along behind him. "Have you found a clue?"

"Just a minute, Geri, there is something I must smell right here," said Pepe, pushing his little body into the hedge until all I could see was the tip of his tail. "If only I could get closer . . ." His voice was muffled by the leaves. Then he disappeared entirely.

And then I heard a splash.

"Pepe?"

There was no answer.

"Pepe?"

Silence.

Then I heard some spluttering and a tiny voice calling out in a watery way: "Help!"

"Pepe!" I tried to push the branches of the hedge aside but with little success.

Once again I heard the tiny voice: "Geri! Help!" and some faint splashing.

I redoubled my efforts. My hands and arms were being scratched, but I finally managed to push aside enough of the branches to see through. The hedge had grown up on either side of a metal fence, and directly on the other side was a huge swimming pool and scrabbling around in the middle of the pool was a small white dog. He didn't seem to be making much progress. In fact, he was so frantic he was making his situation worse. I had to get in there, and I had to get in there fast.

The fence had narrow slats. Pepe had been small enough to squeeze through, but I never could. The only solution was to go up, so I did. I used the stout branches of the hedge for footholds and handholds and scrambled to the top of the fence. From there it was a straight shot down. Into the pool!

With a big splash, I landed beside Pepe.

I scooped him up and did a side stroke with my free arm to the shallow end of the pool. I waded out and set Pepe on the concrete coping. He was spluttering and shivering but otherwise seemed fine.

I, on the other hand, was a mess. My shoes squished with every step I took. My blouse was plastered to my body. My hair was dripping. And worse yet, I knew there was no way out. Looking at the fence from this side, I could see that I could not possibly scale it without the helpful support of the hedge.

And at that moment, I heard a voice: "Hey, what are you doing here?"

I whirled around, flinging water about like a wet dog, and saw Rodney Klamp.

He had just emerged from the back door of the large gray mansion, with a frosted glass in one hand and a purple towel in another. He was wearing a pair of baggy khaki shorts and a purple and green Hawaiian shirt. His sunglasses covered half of his face, but his porcupine hairstyle was distinctive.

"What are you doing here?" I asked.

"I live here," he said, and plunked his glass down on one of the small tables that punctuated the long line of lounge chairs beside the pool. He repeated his question: "What are you doing here?"

"We came by to look at the house and pay our respects to Nigel." I thought that was a nice touch. In fact, I had noticed with surprise that there were no gawkers or floral tributes outside the gates as would be usual when a celebrity dies. Perhaps they had been left at the gates to the studio. "And then my dog fell into the pool by accident."

"Not by accident," said Pepe with a mighty sneeze. "It was a clever diversion to get into the grounds. Ask him for a towel!"

"Can I have a towel to dry him off?"

"Of course," said Rodney, handing over his

purple towel. It appeared to be part of his nature to be helpful. "You can use this one. I'll go get another." He headed back into the house.

I took the towel and began rubbing Pepe down. He made grunting noises that were halfway between complaint and pleasure as I worked over his little body. Finally I just wrapped him up, like a baby in swaddling, and plunked him down on one of the lounge chairs. Rodney had returned with two new towels. "I suppose you need one, too," he observed.

"Thank you." I took the towel and used it to dry my hair. There wasn't much I could do about the rest of me.

"So you jumped in to rescue him?" Rodney said.

"I was afraid he would drown," I said.

"I thought all dogs could dog paddle," Rodney said.

"You would think so," I said. "But even if he made it to the side, I wasn't sure he could get out of the pool."

"Unless he was smart enough to swim to the shallow end and just walk up the steps," Rodney observed.

"Yes, too bad he wasn't that smart," I said, looking at Pepe.

Pepe wriggled out of the towels, stood up, and studied the pool. "It is hard to see exactly where the steps are when you are floundering in the deep end," he said. He looked over at Rodney. "Ask him how long he has lived here."

"So how long have you lived here?" I asked.

"Ever since I was hired. Nigel wanted me to be available twenty-four seven."

"And now?"

"What do you mean?"

"Well . . ." I didn't want to be rude. "Nigel obviously doesn't need you anymore."

"True," said Rodney, "but someone has to answer the phone and go through the mail. Leo, that's Nigel's manager, asked me to stay until they settle the estate."

"I imagine it's substantial," I said, looking up at the house, which loomed over us: all gray stone walls and stained-glass windows and turrets with conical roofs.

"That's what you'd think, but they're about to foreclose on the house. Nigel was completely broke."

"What about all that money he made as the judge on *So You Wanna Be a Star?*"

"It went straight up his nose. Nigel hasn't paid any bills in months. Leo told him he had to get a job. That's why he agreed to be a judge for *Dancing with Dogs.* He didn't want to do it. He thought it was beneath him."

"Hey!" said Pepe. "I have seen *So You Wanna Be a Star. Dancing with Dogs* is a step up!"

"So how was he paying you?"

"He wasn't," said Rodney with a grimace. "But he gave me a place to stay." He pointed at the pool house, a miniature version of the big house, which sat at the end of the pool. He picked up his drink from the table and took a sip. "Do you want something to drink?"

"Sure," I said, thinking it would take me a while to dry out, and it might be pleasant to sit in the sun and have a drink. Besides, as Pepe had pointed out, we were supposed to be investigating. Maybe we would learn something important about Nigel.

"What would you like?" asked Rodney, always the helpful assistant.

"Whatever you're drinking is fine with me," I said. Rodney trotted off to the main house and soon came back with another frosty glass.

"I see he did not think to ask my preference," Pepe said.

"What is your preference?" I asked.

"Water, neat, no chaser, please," he said.

"Can I have a bowl of water for my dog?" I asked.

Rodney went back into the house again. Meanwhile, Pepe wandered over to the base of the wrought-iron table at one end of the pool and lifted his leg.

"Hey!" I said. "That's not cool!"

"I am merely letting the other dog know I am top dog."

"What other dog?" I asked.

Pepe sniffed around the base of the table. "The *perro* that lives here."

Rodney returned carrying a gilt-rimmed china bowl filled with water.

"Does Nigel have a dog?" I asked.

Rodney frowned. "No! What makes you say that?"

"Oh, I don't know." I couldn't really explain that my dog told me so.

Rodney set the bowl down beside the lounge chairs. Pepe sniffed it and then turned away.

"You asked for it!" I said.

"It is always better when it has had a little time to breathe," Pepe said.

He went off on another sniffing expedition, this time along the edge of the trimmed hedges by the kitchen door. "Ah, the scent is very strong here. Yes, there was definitely another *perro* here. Maybe two days ago."

"You're sure Nigel didn't have a dog?" I asked.

"No!" Rodney sat down on a lounge chair and waved me to a seat. "What is it with you people and dogs? Just because you like them doesn't mean everyone in the world does."

Pepe jumped up beside me on the lounge chair and gave my drink a sniff. "Ah!" he said. "This is the smell I smelled at the murder scene. I would recognize it anywhere."

I took a sip. It was a strong gin and tonic. One of my favorite summer drinks.

"Nigel was drinking gin and tonic?" I asked.

Rodney almost dropped the glass he was holding.

"How do you know that?" he asked.

"I just recognize the smell," I said.

"It is I who recognized the smell!" said Pepe.

"Well, you can't tell anyone that Nigel was drinking!" Rodney told me.

"What? Why?"

"Nigel was supposed to be sober," Rodney

said. "We met in rehab. But he just couldn't handle having other people tell him what to do. He managed to convince Leo to let him do rehab on his own at home. So Leo hired me to be his watchdog, so to speak."

"Not a very good one," Pepe observed. "I am a much better watchdog."

"I was supposed to make sure none of his druggy buddies could get to him."

"But drinking was OK?" I asked.

"Well, you know. He slipped a little." Rodney waved his glass in the air. "So did I. But as long as he wasn't doing drugs, I figured I was doing my job."

"So is that why you were worried about leaving him alone?"

"Yes, as soon as he got his advance for *Dancing with Dogs,* he started sneaking around, making phone calls and hanging up when I came in the room. I thought he was trying to score some drugs. That's why I was so worried when I left him alone at the studio."

"Did you tell the police this?" I asked.

Rodney shook his head vigorously. "No, and you can't either." His voice went high with anxiety. "Leo would cut me off without a cent if he knew any of this."

"What do you mean?"

"I mean that Leo promised me a big bonus to be paid at the end of six months if Nigel stayed sober. It was only a week away when he died. If Leo finds out that Nigel was drinking or buying drugs, he won't pay me. And I *need* that money!"

"Because you need to find a new place to live?" I asked.

"No," Rodney said. "One of my friends made a film based on my screenplay. We've got a chance to enter it in Sundance, but we need to finish it within a week. If I don't get that bonus, we're out of luck."

"Everyone in L.A. is in the movie business," Pepe muttered.

Chapter 9

My shoes were still squishing as I headed toward the car with Pepe.

"Perhaps you should not drive when you are all wet, Geri. It could be dangerous," he said.

"What can I do?" I said. "You want to walk all the way back to the hotel?"

"That does not sound good, either," he said.

"Let's just get in the car and go," I told him.

As I dug into my purse for the car keys, he said, "Say, I may have a solution for your wet clothes."

"What's that?"

"It is how Conchita took care of a similar problem in one episode of—"

"How is one of your Spanish soap operas going to help me?"

"Easy," said Pepe. "Conchita was running away from the evil Fernando and fell in the river. When Fernando could not find her, she got out all soaking wet."

"And?"

"She went to a nearby gas station restroom, took all her wet clothes off, and dried them under the hand dryer—you know, those things on the wall that blow hot air out to dry your hands."

"You're kidding!"

"No. It worked. We just need to find a gas station."

"Not happening," I told him. "I'm not going to stand around naked in some public bathroom trying to dry my clothes!"

"It worked for Conchita."

"I'm not Conchita. Get in the car. We're leaving."

"*As you wish*," he said, hopping into the front passenger seat when I opened the door.

"Look on the bright side of things," Pepe told me as I started the car. "At least our investigation is proceeding apace."

"Oh, I forgot to ask Rodney about the package!" I said as we pulled away from the curb. "But I guess I can ask him tomorrow. And it's true—we did learn some new things about Nigel."

"*Sí*, it seems that he was planning to buy drugs at the time he was killed."

"But surely he couldn't have drugs delivered to him at the studio?"

Pepe snorted. "Are you kidding?" he said.

"What do you mean?" I asked him, annoyed at his superior attitude.

"I have been on many a Hollywood set, Geri," Pepe said. "They are crawling with drugs."

"OK, if you say so." I had to give him that. I

had never been on a set before. "But why would someone who wanted to sell him drugs kill him?"

"Perhaps because he owed them money?"

"But surely it would have been smarter to wait, since he was about to begin earning money again," I pointed out.

"But that would go quickly if he returned to his old habits," Pepe pointed out.

It seemed we had reached a dead end. I started to ease the car back into the traffic on Sunset Boulevard.

"Geri, can you stop at a 7-Eleven? All this investigating has left me famished."

"I kind of doubt there are any 7-Elevens in Beverly Hills, Pepe."

"Wait!" he suddenly exclaimed, his nose sniffing like mad. "I smell something!"

"Don't tell me, you smell a 7-Eleven?"

"No, it is something else."

"What?"

"Turn right here," he said.

"What?"

"Right, right," he repeated. "Right on this street."

I almost missed the corner but did as he asked.

"Now what? What are we doing?"

"Turn right again!"

I turned.

"Now left!" Pepe said after we'd gone a couple blocks.

I followed his directions once again and ended up going down a wide, tree-lined street that serpentined past luxury mansion after mansion, most set well back from the road.

"Slow down!" Pepe commanded, his nose sniffing a mile a minute.

Instead of slowing, I pulled over to the curb and stopped, saying, "I'm not going any farther until you tell me what we're doing."

He turned and faced me. "Geri, *por favor*, just a little more. It is *muy importante*!" He stuck his nose back out of the car and took a deep breath. "Ah, *sí*," he said like some particular odor was instantly recognizable. All I could smell was the scent of freshly mowed lawns.

"Move the car forward, Geri," said Pepe. "Slowly! We are almost there."

This seemed so important to my pooch that I gave the car a little gas, and we crept forward at about ten miles per hour.

"Even slower!" Pepe said after we'd gone less than a hundred feet.

Down to five miles per hour.

"Slower still!"

Down to two miles per hour, barely a crawl.

"*¡Alto!*" he told me. "This is it!"

"This is *what*?" I asked, applying the brakes.

"Ah, the *hacienda* of my youth," he said, his tail wagging furiously. "I would recognize its sweet smell anywhere!"

"What? Where?" I asked, looking past his nose. I couldn't see anything but an eight-foot-tall hedge like the one at Nigel's house.

"Move the car up to the gate," Pepe told me. "You will see."

Rolling forward a bit, I stopped at a short

driveway between the hedges. There, beyond a wide, wrought-iron gate, was a magnificent, Spanish-style mansion, two stories high with white stucco walls and a red-tile roof. A number of cars were parked in the circular driveway.

"This is where you grew up?" I asked my dog.

"*Sí*," he said. "It is the *casa* of Caprice Kennedy."

"We're at Caprice's house?"

"Of course, Geri. It is what I smelled. One does not forget meaningful odors—especially the happy ones."

I could hardly believe it. We must have driven close to a mile since Pepe first noticed the scent of Caprice's place. If this was Caprice's place. I pulled out my Map of the Stars and began looking for a star with Caprice's name on it.

After a few moments, Pepe said, "Well?"

"Well what?" I looked up from my map. The star that marked the home of Caprice Kennedy did seem to be in the general area where we had stopped. Perhaps Pepe had sneaked a look at the map.

"Are you not going to pull up to the gate so we can go in?"

"Pepe, why would they let us in?"

"Because they know me," he said.

I shook my head. "Pepe, even if this is the right house—"

"Just pull forward," he said. "There is a radio intercom there. I can talk them into admitting us."

Well, maybe I could dissuade Pepe from his

delusions by going along with him. "OK," I said. "Why not?"

At the gate, there was indeed an intercom mounted at the driver's side of the car. I pressed the button, and it was only a couple seconds before I heard a male voice, deep and sonorous. "Who is it?"

"Hi, uh, I'm Geri Sullivan," I said.

"Yes?" asked the man.

"Tell Caprice that Pepe has returned!" said Pepe.

"Is that a dog with you?" he asked.

"Yes," I said.

"Oh, you must be with the dog show. Come on in!" the man said. "The party is out back by the pool." And the gate began to glide open.

"You see, Geri!" said Pepe as we cruised up the driveway. "Caprice has not forgotten me."

Chapter 10

"You know, Pepe," I told him, "it sounds like she's having a party."

"Caprice is always throwing parties," he said. "She is famous for them."

Caprice had a lot of guests, judging from the line of cars parked in front of the house. I found a spot at the end of the line for my rented red convertible.

"This way, Geri!" said Pepe, jumping out of the car and charging around the corner of the house. I followed behind him somewhat reluctantly. Unlike Pepe, I'm not good at parties. And I felt even more awkward than usual because we were crashing this one. Plus I was still dealing with the consequences of falling in the pool. My damp jeans had molded themselves to my legs, as wet jeans will do. And although my yellow cotton blouse was mostly dry—thank God it was no longer transparent—my hair had scrunched up into ringlets all over my head. Not the most fashionable look for a party at the home of a movie star.

Pepe had no such concerns. He dived right into the crowd of people gathered around the huge swimming pool, in the back of the house, which had been landscaped, complete with waterfall, giant boulders, and lush foliage, to create the illusion that we were in some sort of tropical paradise.

Fortunately, I saw right away that this was a *Dancing with Dogs* party. A TV screen was set up on the terrace, shaded by a striped awning. Scenes from the show flashed across the screen. The German shepherd leaping through a hoop held by his owner. The three judges conferring, their heads together. The poodle, his little pompoms jiggling as he pranced around the stage. Rebecca stood near the screen with a silver-haired man, possibly the cinematographer. She was watching the images and gesturing with her hands. The guy leaned back with his arms crossed across his chest.

A bar was set up by the back door, and most of the guests held drinks in their hands. I thought I recognized some of the camera guys and lighting techs, but I didn't see any of the other contestants, or choreographers, or dogs. Or Pepe, either. Where was he?

I finally located him in the crowd of young men gathered around Caprice. As I approached, he was telling her, "Caprice, you will be so proud of me! I found our house by smelling it!"

Our house. Those words pierced my heart.

Caprice stopped midsentence. She wore a formfitting, blindingly white cotton dress with some strategic cutouts, which provided plenty of glimpses of her tanned flesh. "I swear that dog is talking to me!" she said with a little laugh.

"I am talking to you, Caprice!" said Pepe.

She looked down at him, and I held my breath. Could she hear him, too?

Then she smiled and said, "Oh, I know who you are! You're the Chihuahua from the show." She raised her head, and I thought for a moment she was looking for me. But instead she called out, "Jennifer!"

A dark-haired young woman, who was dressed in black jeans and a black tank top, stepped out from the shadows behind a palm tree, where she had apparently been waiting for such a command. She presented herself in front of Caprice.

Caprice picked up Pepe and kissed him on the head. "He looks like the dog I used to have," she said with a wistful tone in her voice. "Do you remember that dog, Jennifer?"

"Yes," Jennifer said. She bent her head so her straight hair fell forward and covered her face.

"Don't you think he looks like my Pepe?" She cradled him in the crook of her arm and rocked him like a baby.

"I am your Pepe!" said Pepe.

"No," said Jennifer with only a cursory look at him. "This dog is much fatter and older."

"You are fatter and older, too!" snarled Pepe, raising his head and growling a little.

"I guess you're right," said Caprice with a sad

tone in her voice. "Anyway, he shouldn't be out here. It's not safe. Someone might step on him! Take him and put him with the other dogs." She handed him to Jennifer, who carried him away, holding him at arm's length. Pepe was twisting and turning, trying to get back to Caprice. I think he had forgotten about me altogether.

I tried to catch up with Jennifer, but she knew her way around. She dodged the guests and skirted the patio furniture and disappeared into the back door of Caprice's mansion. I followed her through a sunroom, down a wide hall, and down a set of narrow stairs. Where was she taking Pepe? To some sort of basement dungeon? Oddly enough, Pepe was quiet and calm.

We passed a wall covered with publicity photos of Caprice. I thought I saw one of her posing with Pepe. It seemed Caprice only used the dogs for photo opportunities but locked them up when they didn't serve her public image. Ahead of me, Jennifer turned a corner and I hurried after her.

Around the corner, the hall opened up into a huge playroom, covered with AstroTurf and littered with dog toys. High windows on one wall let in natural light and the scent of eucalyptus and chlorine. I could hear the murmur of the guests in the pool area.

There were lots of little dogs scampering around the room, doing the things dogs usually do, dashing at each other and sniffing each other's butts. I recognized a few of them: Caprice's Papillon, Princess, still wearing her diamond collar, and Siren Song, the golden

Pomeranian, Pepe's lady love. The rest were small dogs: a toy poodle, a silky gray shih tzu with a topknot, and even a Puli, one of those funny dogs that look like a mop, but no other Chihuahuas.

Jennifer set Pepe down behind a baby gate that blocked the door.

"Home sweet home!" he announced with great satisfaction, and went scampering off to join the other dogs.

"Nasty little creature!" said Jennifer, brushing off her hands as if to rid them of contaminants.

"Don't you like dogs?" I asked.

"Oh!" she said when she turned and saw me behind her. She threw up her hands, as if to ward me off. "You scared me."

"That's my dog you just brought down here."

"Yes, well, Caprice asked me to bring him down here." Jennifer sounded defensive. "She worries about the dogs when there are so many people around. She wants them to stay here where they won't get stepped on or fall in the pool."

So Caprice was actually a responsible dog owner. I didn't like hearing that any more than I liked hearing Pepe describe this place as his "home." But I could see his point. It was dog heaven. There was even a little kitchen in the corner of the room. Stainless-steel bowls of water were set out on the linoleum, and glass jars of treats lined the counter.

"You don't like dogs?" I repeated my question.

"Dogs are OK," Jennifer said. She brushed back a lock of hair with her wrist. "It's just not fair. They have their own personal chef who prepares fresh-cooked meals with organic vegetables and free-range meat. A trainer comes in to work with them three days a week, and a groomer comes once a week to do their hair and nails. And what do we get?" She looked at me with her eyes squinted.

"None of that?"

"That's right. We're on call twenty-four hours a day. And she almost always calls me when I'm on a date or at the gym. And acting classes or auditions? Forget it! She seems to have a sixth sense about when I'm really serious about my career and she'll do anything to keep me down."

"So you're an actress?"

"Yes, I got a part in a small independent film, but every time the director schedules a shoot or a voice-over, Caprice comes up with something else I need to do instead, like taking the dogs to the doggie spa. I think she's trying to sabotage my career."

"How long have you worked for Caprice?" I asked.

"Three years," Jennifer said.

"So do you remember the other little white Chihuahua she had?" I asked. I glanced at my little white Chihuahua. He had circled the entire playroom, sniffing each object and often nodding his head, as if to say, "Yes, I remember this!"

Jennifer nodded, her eyes down.

"So are you sure this isn't the same dog?"

"Absolutely!" She looked up at that and shook her long straight hair like a pony getting rid of a fly.

"How can you be so sure?"

"Look," she said, grabbing my arm with sharp fingernails. "That other dog died. He ran out into the street and was hit by a car. We just didn't tell Caprice because we knew she would be devastated. So we told her he ran away."

"Oh!" I looked over at my dog again. He had finished with his inspection of the room and was now greeting the other dogs in typical dog fashion. He began by sniffing under the tail of his lady love, Siren Song, and she returned the favor.

I couldn't imagine what life would be like if anything ever happened to him.

I heard a shrill ringing sound, and Jennifer jumped. She pulled a cell phone out of her pocket and looked at it. "Caprice wants me," she said. "Gotta go!"

"I'll just stay and watch my dog for a minute," I said. "Sometimes he doesn't get along with other dogs."

That was an understatement. Pepe regularly challenged dogs twice his size. In Seattle, he had antagonized a Great Dane, which turned out to be to my benefit, as I got to meet the dog's handsome trainer, Felix Navarro. We had just started dating when I left Seattle, and it was hard to be away from him, though some distance was probably good. I have a pretty poor track record at picking men.

I was bumped out of my reverie by the sound of high-pitched barking. Pepe had gone right up to Princess and backed her into a corner. She was giving as good as she got, snapping and yipping right back at him. I was about to intervene when their tones changed. They began circling each other, tails wagging. How odd! Pepe and Princess had been foes since they first met. Then Pepe's ears drooped and his tail curled under. My brave little man was being cowed by the prissy Princess.

He came running over to me and whimpered a little. I had never seen my dog in such an emotional state. I picked him up and cuddled him.

"Pepe, what's the matter? Are you all right?"

"No," he said softly.

"What is it?"

"Well, I was challenging her for that big pink doggy bed in the corner. That used to be mine." I looked and saw that Princess had indeed settled down on the bed in question, which was designed to look like a four-poster, complete with canopy.

"Really, it's too girly for you, Pepe," I said.

"It had blue covers and blue satin sheets in my day," he said. "Geri, pay attention. This is *importante*. I was talking to Princess—"

"Do you mean you were really talking to her?"

"*Sí*, but not as I talk to you, of course," he said, sounding a little annoyed. At least he perked up. "With us *perros*, it is a complex language: the twitch of the fur, the wrinkle of the muzzle, the scent of the skin, the gleam in the eye. Far too subtle for a human."

"So what's wrong?"

"It is what Princess told me," he said. His big brown eyes seemed to be full of tears.

"What did she tell you?"

"She said the bed used to belong to Caprice's favorite dog, Pepe. Caprice always cries when she talks about him. She loved him very much, but he ran away and left her. Princess says it broke Caprice's heart!"

Chapter 11

Pepe was still trembling when we arrived back at the Chateau Marmont. I tucked him into my bed and sat beside him until he fell asleep. Then I got up and turned on my laptop. I had to solve the mystery of Caprice's white Chihuahua. I had been hearing this story from Pepe ever since I adopted him, but I had never thought to do any research.

Typing the words *Caprice, Pepe,* and *Chihuahua* into a search engine brought up a wealth of links, including photos of Caprice clutching a white Chihuahua and cuddling a white Chihuahua and even shopping with a white Chihuahua tucked into her purse.

What was more disturbing were the news stories about how Caprice's dog had run away last October, about six months before I adopted Pepe from a Seattle shelter. She was offering a $50,000 reward for his return. But what about Jennifer's story? It made more sense that

Caprice's little white Chihuahua had been killed since no one had ever claimed the reward.

I sighed. I didn't know who to believe. Pepe had told me dozens of outrageous stories, each one more unbelievable than the last. He had worked for the DEA; he had traveled in France; he had been a junkyard dog in Tijuana. He watched a lot of TV. I suspected his little brain had been addled by too many Spanish soap operas and true-crime TV shows.

It was totally possible he had seen the news about Caprice's dog on the news and had invented a story that made him the lost heir. I had similar fantasies when I was a child—thinking I was a princess whose royal parents would eventually come to reclaim her from the peasants they had asked to raise her.

I shut down my laptop. Although it was late, I decided to call Felix. We had only been out three times back in Seattle, and I was still unsure of his intentions toward me, although I was quite clear about my intentions toward him. Unfortunately, Pepe sensed these intentions and did his best to sabotage my attempts to lure Felix into my bed. So we hadn't progressed much beyond a few steamy kisses at my front door, which meant I didn't really know if calling this late at night was appropriate. Perhaps he had another girlfriend. Perhaps he lived with her. All I had was his cell phone number, which he used to stay in touch with his dog-training clients.

I couldn't find my cell phone, so I called him on the phone in the room. It rang and rang and then went to voice mail. I listened to Felix's sexy voice for a moment: "Hello, this is Felix Navarro, dog wrangler. If you have need of my services, let me know." Ah, yes, I needed his services, but not to wrangle my dog, who was behaving himself for once. Pepe had burrowed under the covers on my bed and was snoring quietly. I loved to listen to him snore. It was the tiniest sound, so adorable.

I left Felix a message: "Thinking of you. Hope all is going well. Call me if you get a chance." As I turned away to get ready for bed, the phone began ringing. I snatched it up. It was Felix. He sounded breathless.

"Geri! I'm so glad you called. I've been trying to reach you all day."

"Really?"

"Yes, your cell goes straight to voice mail."

"That's odd. I was just looking for it and couldn't find it. Maybe it's at the bottom of Nigel St. Nigel's pool."

"What were you doing in Nigel St. Nigel's pool?"

"Well, Pepe wanted to investigate."

"Of course he did." Felix sounded amused; then his voice got serious. "But, Geri, I heard about the murder. You need to be careful. I'm sure Nigel St. Nigel had some powerful enemies."

"Yes, well, that's why I'm leaving it to the police." I paused. "And you? How are you?"

His voice got vague. "Oh, I've been really busy."

"Lots of dogs to wrangle?"

"More than usual. I had to double up on clients

because I've got a big gig at the end of the week that's going to take me out of town."

"Oh, where are you going?"

"No place exciting," he said.

"Well, where?" I suddenly got self-conscious. "Or am I not supposed to ask?" Was there another woman in the picture? I hadn't really learned much about his romantic past.

"Oh, you can ask, but I can't tell." He laughed, but it was an awkward laugh. "Actually it's just an old client who lives in California and wants to fly me down for some private lessons." It was clear he didn't want to talk about it. Maybe he did have another girlfriend. Or *a* girlfriend. Maybe I wasn't a girlfriend at all. "So, Geri, you called for a reason?"

How did he know that? I wanted to protest that I called just to hear his sexy voice, but I felt a little too vulnerable to do that. "Yes, I'm wondering about Pepe."

"Is he having problems?" Felix had been eager to train Pepe ever since we first met, but Pepe was having none of it.

"Not any more than usual," I said. "It's about his background." How could I explain that Pepe thought he was Caprice's long-lost dog? I had not yet been able to tell Felix about Pepe's talking. I thought of Ted, who would understand, but he wouldn't know the answer to my question.

"What is it, Geri?'

"Well, Caprice used to have a little white Chihuahua that looked a lot like Pepe. He disappeared about six months before I adopted Pepe.

Do you think Pepe could be her dog? He *was* originally from L.A."

"I doubt it." Felix sounded very sure of himself. "There must be hundreds of white Chihuahuas in L.A."

"How would I know for sure?"

"Well, he's chipped, isn't he?"

"I don't know."

"They would have certainly checked for a chip at the shelter. If the chip identified his owner, they would have returned him."

"But what if he doesn't have a chip?"

"That's unlikely. Almost all dogs are chipped these days when they pass through a shelter. That's where you got him, right?"

"Yes, he had been abandoned in a shelter in L.A., and they flew him and a bunch of other Chihuahuas up to a shelter in Seattle."

"So if he wasn't chipped when he arrived, they would have chipped him at the shelter."

"Odd. I don't remember them giving me any information about that."

"Sometimes the vet or the shelter will just register the dog themselves. Then if the dog is lost and found, the number traces back to the shelter or vet and they can contact the owner. The assumption is those businesses might be more stable than the owners who can change addresses or phone numbers frequently."

"How would I find out if Pepe is chipped?"

"Any vet could tell you."

"Oh, there's one on set," I said. "I'll ask her."

"Anyone I know?"

"Do you know all the vets in L.A.?" I asked.

"Just the ones who work in the film business," he replied. Felix had grown up in L.A. and spent years working as an animal trainer on movie sets.

"I think her name is Alice."

"Is she a cute little blonde with blue eyes, about five-two?"

"Yes," I said. That certainly described her.

"Well, if it's Alice Bennett, she's one of the best. You can trust her to take care of your little Chihuahua." His voice got wistful. "I wish I was there to take care of you. I worry about you, Geri."

"There's nothing to worry about," I assured him, though I'm not sure why. I would love to have him taking care of me, though Pepe would surely object. He thought he was taking care of me.

After saying my good-byes to Felix, I got ready for bed and slipped under the covers. Pepe woke up and snuggled closer to me, shaping himself to fit within the curve of my arms.

Back at home in Seattle, I often didn't get to sleep with him because Albert the Cat laid claim to the bed. So it was a special treat when Pepe laid his soft little head on my arm and went back to sleep. I could feel his warm breath on my skin as I drifted off.

Chapter 12

The schedule for the second day was much like the first. A 7:00 a.m. wake-up call, four hours at the dance studio in the morning to learn a new routine, and then off via town car to the soundstage for the afternoon costume fitting, run-through, and filming.

They had designed a cute way of giving us our assignments, which they filmed. We waited in our empty practice room and a little white Maltese came trotting in with a bunch of dog tags around his neck. We chose one and read off the name of our dance. Then our assigned choreographer came in to work with us. Our dance for the second day was hip-hop and our choreographer was a gentleman named Flash Daddy.

In addition, Rebecca announced an extra twist. She had informed the costume designers to make us look as much like our dogs as possible, and the choreographers were supposed to do the same.

"Do not worry, Geri," said Pepe. "We will kick it." And he dropped and did a couple of doggy push-ups.

"How did you learn how to do that?" I asked him.

"Watching TV," he replied. "You can learn everything on TV."

Flash Daddy created a routine for us that featured lots of push-ups and tail wagging, not to mention some side leg lifts. Easy for Pepe, not so easy for me.

"Geri, you need to imagine that there is a fire hydrant on either side of you," Pepe said.

"Pepe, fire hydrants don't really inspire me," I said, pushing my hair out of my face with the back of my wrist.

"And you need to aim high, because a Great Dane was there before you," Pepe went on.

I wrinkled up my nose. "Ugh!"

"Geri," said Pepe solemnly, "there is nothing wrong with marking your territory and marking it well."

"Yes, but by peeing on it?" I asked.

"Do you need a break, Miss Sullivan?" asked Flash Daddy.

"No, I'm good," I said.

"Try getting into character," said Flash Daddy.

"You can be L.L. Cool Geri," said Pepe.

"L.L. Cool Geri?"

"That's a good name!" said Flash Daddy. "That will work."

"And I'll be L'il Dawg," said my little dog.

To my surprise, the name change worked. The rehearsal went much better.

"Let's try it one more time," said Flash Daddy. And so we did. Once, twice, three times.

When we finished, Flash Daddy gave me a fist bump. "You're getting down, girl."

At the soundstage, Shelley, the second assistant director, sent us to the costume room. Robyn and her crew had created a little baseball cap for Pepe that fit over one of his ears, with the brim backward. They also made him a gold chain like all the hip-hop moguls wore. I had a matching baseball cap and gold chain, but the rest of my costume was more elaborate, as I was supposed to look like my dog. Robyn had made me a skintight, white, fake-fur catsuit.

"It should be called a dog suit, not a *gato* suit," Pepe observed.

I turned around to admire my form in the mirror as Robyn pinned a feathery tail to my rear end.

"I will admit they have done a good job on your costume," said Pepe. "You do indeed look like a Chihuahua. But the largest one I have ever seen."

I wasn't entirely sure that was a compliment. You can never tell with Pepe.

Our next stop was makeup. While we were waiting for our turn, Jake, the Certified Animal Safety Representative, strolled up. He was a big, broad man with deeply tanned skin and deep wrinkles around his eyes. He looked like someone who spent a lot of time outside, doing something like fishing or hunting.

He gave me the once-over. "You make a mighty fine dog," he said. "Perhaps I should be keeping my eye on you."

I laughed politely. "How's it going?"

He shrugged. "Everything seems fine. All the dogs are happy." He bent down to pat Pepe on the head, but it was pretty clear that it was just a token gesture. "Cute little feller," he said. "Though I prefer the bigger breeds, myself. Working dogs, you know, that's what dogs were meant to do."

"I work plenty," said Pepe. "Tell him, Geri. Tell him that we are private investigators."

"My dog works pretty hard," I said. "You should see his hip-hop routine."

"Well, I guess I will in an hour or so," Jake said.

"So you watch every performance?" I asked. "What exactly are you looking for?"

"Any physical movements that might put too much stress on the animals," he said. "Dogs have some physical limitations, and certain activities could be dangerous for them."

"People have physical limitations, too," said Pepe. "I can do things that humans cannot do. For instance, lick my own—"

"Never mind, Pepe!" I said sharply.

"For example, the German shepherd," Jake rambled on. "Those dogs are notorious for hip problems and shouldn't be doing any movements that would compromise their hip joints."

"Shouldn't you be watching the rehearsals, then?" I asked. "You could spot problems before the performances."

As soon as I said it, I wished I could take it back. If Jake came to the rehearsals, he'd run into Ted. I had seen him briefly at the dance studio. He told me he was choreographing a Jive routine for the border collie today.

I tried to backpedal. "I'm sure the choreographers are aware of what is in the best interest of the dogs."

"I'm not so sure about that," said Jake. "My contract only requires me to be on the set, but I'll see if I can extend that to the rehearsal space. Thanks for the suggestion."

I smiled weakly. I would have to warn Ted.

"There is one other thing that worries me," said Jake. "I'm afraid they are going to stage some kind of fight. I've insisted they keep the dogs separate, but you know how it is with these reality TV shows. They always have to stir up conflict, and if there isn't any, they create it."

"That would be bad," I agreed. "One of the dogs could get hurt."

"We're ready for you now," said Zack, the stylist.

As we went in, Siren Song and her dance partner, Luis, filed past. Pepe gazed at his lady love with longing eyes. She was all fluffed up with gold glitter sprinkled over her fur and a big gold flounce flapping off one shoulder. Luis had her tucked into the crook of his elbow. He wore a tight silky T-shirt, the same reddish-gold color as the Pomeranian's fur and a pair of tight, gold lamé trousers. They were doing a salsa. They might be our toughest competition for this round.

Pepe was carried off to have a bath and a trim, and I took advantage of his absence to duck into the vet's office. Luckily, Alice was there, paging through a thick book. She put it down and gave me a rueful smile.

"Studying for an exam," she said. "What can I do for you?"

"I'm wondering if my Chihuahua is chipped," I said.

"I can certainly check him out for you. I should be able to tell if he has a chip by just feeling for it. But I won't be able to give you any more information without a scanner. I don't have one here, but I can bring it in tomorrow."

"That would be great," I told her. "And there's one more thing."

"Yes?"

"Do you think you could check him without him knowing it?"

"I doubt that he will know what a scanner is," she said.

"But could we just not say anything about it?" I asked. "Like maybe pretend it's a routine test that all the dogs have to undergo?"

"Whatever you want," she said, but I could tell by her eyes that she thought I was a little nutty. Maybe I was.

* * *

I was still sitting in front of the mirror, watching my stylist pull my hair back into a high ponytail, when Pepe came trotting over, shaking himself with vehemence, the way he always did after being exposed to water. The groomer had placed the little baseball cap over one ear, and the gold chain was firmly positioned in the center of his chest.

"Are we ready, L'il Dawg?" I asked him, getting out of the chair.

"Ready if you are, L.L. Cool Geri!" said Pepe.

Just then Shelley came hurrying up. "You've got a visitor."

"Who?" I asked, looking around but seeing no one.

"Says his name is James Gerrard," she said, looking at her clipboard, "and I really don't have time to deal with this. You're not supposed to have visitors on the set."

"He's my boss back in Seattle. I don't know how he found me."

"Why don't you ask him?" she said, turning around to look behind her. "Now, where did he go? He's not supposed to be loose on the set."

"Jimmy G's right here," said my boss, popping out from behind a screen.

Chapter 13

Jimmy G was hard to miss. He always dresses like a forties detective cliché. And today was no exception. He wore a pair of two-toned brown-and-white loafers, tan slacks with cuffs, a houndstooth sports jacket with extra-wide lapels, and a brown fedora, tipped to a jaunty angle over one eye.

"Hi, doll," he said, giving me the once-over. "Jimmy G almost didn't recognize you in that funny-looking, fuzzy-wuzzy costume you're wearing. What are you supposed to be? A big rabbit?"

"A dog," I told him.

"Well, not too many women would admit to that," he said. He added a "Ha-ha!" since I didn't laugh at his joke.

Jimmy G glanced down at Pepe. "I see the rat-dog's with you as usual."

Pepe responded to the insult with a growl. (I was always amazed when he made actual dog sounds instead of speaking.)

"Same back at ya," my boss told Pepe before

turning his attention back to me. "Jimmy G had a tough time getting in here to see you." He pointed at Shelley, adding, "This hard-nosed broad kept trying to send me to a different soundstage."

"They're remaking *Kiss of Death* on Soundstage 12," said Shelley. "I thought you were one of the extras."

"Hey, do you think there's any chance of that?" Jimmy G's face lit up. "Might as well get a little camera action. When in Hollywood, do as the natives do!"

"You'd have to ask them," Shelley said with a sour face. She turned to me, clutching her clipboard. "You're not supposed to have visitors on set unless you notify me in advance. So I can't allow this guy to remain."

"I'm sorry," I said. "I didn't know he was going to show up here. How did you find us anyway?"

Jimmy G gave a snort. "Whadda ya think? Jimmy G's a private eye. Tracked you down!" He seemed mighty proud of himself. "So where's this package?"

Oh, the package. I had completely forgotten about it. "It must be around here someplace," I said. "I gave it to Rodney for safekeeping."

"Who's Rodney?"

"Rodney Klamp. He's the assistant to the assistant to the assistant director. But I haven't seen him today. Where is he?" I turned to Shelley.

"He never showed up this morning," said Shelley.

"So this guy who's disappeared is the last

person who had Jimmy G's package?" Jimmy G
was getting agitated. "He probably stole it."

"Why would he do that?" I asked. "What was in
it, anyway?"

"Jimmy G's not at liberty to say. It's important,
that's all. Very important."

"We can look around for it," I told him.

"No, you can't!" said Shelley. "You're supposed to be onstage in five minutes. We're on a
very tight schedule."

"Do you know how to get a hold of this
Rodney character?" Jimmy G asked Shelley.

She shook her head. "No." She gave Jimmy G
a shove. "Now, you! Get out of here! And, you
two!" She pointed at me and Pepe. "Onstage!
Now!" She stormed away, clutching her clipboard.

"Jimmy G has to find this guy," said our boss,
his big brown eyes rolling.

"You could try him at his house," I said. "We
were there last night. Well, not really his house,
but where he's staying." I dug the Map of the
Stars out of my purse and showed Jimmy G
the location of Nigel's house. As he took off, I
heard him mutter, "Nacho, damned Nacho."

Our second performance went a little more
smoothly than our first. Rebecca announced us
as "L.L. Cool Geri" and "L'il Dawg," and I slid
ever so comfortably into character. Pepe and
I punched and kicked through our hip-hop
routine, gaining confidence and energy as we
danced. I crouched down and he jumped over

me. I did imagine all the fire hydrants as we did our side leg lifts in perfect unison. Then he crouched down and I jumped over him. The audience howled.

When L'il Dawg and I finished and took our bows, even the judges went wild. The audience was on their feet, and I thought I saw Jimmy G in the front row.

"You rocked it, L.L. Cool Geri!" said Pepe.

"So did you, L'il Dawg!" I said, giving him a low five.

Miranda gave us a ten, Beverly gave us a nine, and Caprice gave us an eight. Her comment: "Although the routine was cute, I've seen better dancing at my parties." Still our score was high enough for us to bump Siren Song and Luis out of their current spot in first place.

We headed to the interview room to wait for the results, which were disappointing. The poodle Max, who had danced last, got a perfect score and came in first, acing us out by only one point. Siren Song had taken third place.

Then we went back through hair and makeup. By the time we got into our street clothes— jeans and a tank top for me, fur for Pepe—the set was almost deserted. The lights were low as we picked our way toward the glowing exit sign.

As we approached the door, I saw a shadow peel itself away from the wall. For a moment, I was frightened. After all, we didn't know who had killed Nigel St. Nigel. But then I realized it was Ted Messenger.

"Hi, I was waiting for you," he said. "I wanted to compliment you. You did great tonight. I

know you'll be able to take the lead again."
He held open the door so we could walk out.
The sky was bright after the darkness of the
soundstage.

"Thanks!" I paused and shaded my eyes so I
could see his face. "You know, I should warn you
that I talked to Jake, the Animal Safety Representative, and I think, because of something I said,
he might show up for the morning rehearsals."

"So?"

"That might be a problem for you."

"It might be," said Ted. He didn't seem concerned. "But I might not be there in the morning, anyway."

"Oh, that's too bad." I kept my tone light,
though I was disappointed. "I was hoping we
would get a chance to work with you again."

"Geri, I think you should ask this dude out!"
said Pepe.

"Why wouldn't you be here tomorrow morning?" I asked Ted.

"The choreography bit isn't getting me the
access I need to all the dogs. I've got to find
another way to roam freely around the set."

We were heading down the alley between the
soundstages, toward the parking lot. A guy carrying a plastic tree over his shoulder walked by us.

"He might have seen something outside the
soundstage that will help us figure out who
murdered Nigel," said Pepe.

"Have you heard anything more from the
police?" I asked.

"No. I assume my lawyer has that all under
control. Have you heard from him?"

"No," I said, but then I remembered my cell phone might be at the bottom of Nigel's pool. Maybe it was ringing underwater.

"But what did he see?" asked Pepe.

"Do you remember seeing anyone around, right before you picked up the gun?" I asked.

"Are you still sleuthing?" he asked.

"Sleuthing? What sleuthing?" I asked with a little laugh.

We had reached the parking lot, and I didn't see the town car that usually took us back to the hotel.

"I've seen you talking to everyone," he said. "You're trying to figure out who killed Nigel, aren't you?"

"Of course we are," said Pepe. "We are detectives!"

"Well, if I did find anything," I said, "I would tell the police." Then I realized that might sound like a threat to the guy who was a suspect. "But we haven't. Found anything, that is."

"Cute, how you keep talking about your dog as if he is your partner," said Ted.

"I am her partner!" said Pepe.

He saw me looking around the parking lot. "Do you need a ride back to your hotel?"

"I would love a ride," I said.

"Great!" He pointed out his car: a sleek, black Jaguar convertible.

"Sweet!" Pepe said when he saw the sporty car. "I call shotgun."

"How does an animal activist get a fancy car like this?" I asked as I settled into the passenger seat. Pepe sat on my lap. Felix would have insisted that he ride in the back, but in a convertible, what did it matter? If we got into an accident, Pepe would fly out of the car like a furry football. The thought made me grab him tighter.

"I get paid well for what I do," said Ted absently as he exited the studio lot and nosed the car out into the L.A. traffic. "Have you had much time for sightseeing since you've been here?"

"Not really," I said. "We've been too busy. Dancing and sleuthing."

"Well, I think you should see some iconic L.A. sights. How about a trip to the beach?"

"Sure, we'd love that!" I said. "Wouldn't we, Pepe?"

"I do not enjoy the beach," said Pepe. "The sand gets between my sensitive toes."

Chapter 14

Everyone in L.A. seemed to be heading west. Santa Monica Boulevard was a sluggish river of cars. But Ted seemed to know what he was doing. He turned left, zigzagged through a series of curving streets lined with oleander hedges, and eventually we popped out onto a wide boulevard. The ocean lay before us, a heavy gray mass exhaling white-topped waves. Ted pulled into a parking lot, and we climbed out of the car.

We passed an outdoor area where muscle-bound men were working out and past a vacant lot filled with booths that were selling colorful T-shirts, and kites, and sunglasses. We headed north up a winding boardwalk, dodging roller skaters and cyclists. A brown-skinned man in a white turban skated up to us, playing an electric guitar strapped to an amplifier on his back. His pale blue eyes were portals into some fantastic world.

"Harry Perry," said Ted. "Everybody knows

him." He veered off the path and onto the sand, heading toward the water's edge. Sand filtered in through the spaces in my sandals, and I stopped and peeled them off. Pepe was not happy. He lifted his little feet high in the air, grumbling the whole time.

Ted got far ahead of us. I could see his lanky form, his long lean legs in those tight jeans. He faced the ocean with his arms spread and put his head back so the light fell on his upturned face. It was such a private moment I wanted to turn away, but then he spun around and came racing back to me.

"Isn't this glorious?" he said.

I could see what he meant. The sun was setting over the sea, and there was a path of gold, right in front of us, sparkling on the water. But as I looked around, my mood darkened. The sand was littered with trash. And a gang of ugly seagulls huddled a few yards away, shrieking at Pepe. They looked big enough and mean enough to carry him off. The breeze was brisk, throwing stinging sand in our faces. Very few people were sunbathing, but the surfers were out, in wet suits, slipping and sliding down the surfaces of the waves.

"Did I tell you about how I learned to surf?" Pepe asked.

I shook my head.

"It was with Caprice," he said. "She had to learn to surf for her role in *Beach Baby,* and she took me along to her lessons. I can hang twenty with the best of them."

"How did you learn to surf if you're afraid of the water?" I asked.

"I'm not afraid of the water," said Ted, coming over to me.

But Pepe did not respond. Unusual. I wondered if I had finally caught him in a lie, and then I wondered if all his stories were lies. Maybe he needed to make himself look big by making up these fantastic tales because he was such a little dog.

"Let's sit here," said Ted, drawing me over to a spot on the sand. He spread his jacket out on the sand. We hunkered down, and he flung his arm around me, I think to warm me up because it didn't seem like a romantic gesture.

The sun turned bloodred. I shivered and Ted drew me closer. Pepe managed to wriggle in between us and planted himself so that my leg would not brush up against Ted's, all without saying a word, remarkable for him. He continued to gaze out at the sunset as if he were meditating.

"What about you?" I asked Ted. "Found any evidence of dog abuse?"

Ted stiffened. "It might sound funny to you, but it's not amusing to me. Dogs don't exist to entertain us."

"But there's a system in place to make sure they're not being abused."

"I'm not talking about that," said Ted. "We treat them like servants. But they are beings with their own cultures. Do you know that whales pass along their favorite songs? And elephants mourn their dead. And dogs know when another member of their pack has died, even over a great distance. They are sentient beings. They have things to teach us, if only we could listen."

"See!" said Pepe. "You are lucky I am around to teach you!"

That began a long rant in which Ted envisioned a world where even rivers and trees had rights and lawyers represented them in court when they were threatened with being covered over or chopped down. It was quite a vision and I enjoyed it.

As Ted was waxing poetic, Pepe took off chasing the seagulls that had been gathering around us like a crowd of creepy stalkers. The light was going out of the sky, and the surfers left the water one by one.

"You never told me about how you got involved in PETA," I told Ted when he stopped to take a breath. "You started to tell me once." Pepe came back, having driven the seagulls back, and sat in my lap.

"Oh," Ted said, and he stiffened. "It was something that happened when I was in college. I was a psych major, and I got a work study job in the Psych Department. I was pretty excited, as you can imagine—a job in my field—but my job was to feed the chimpanzees. They were using them for research, trying to determine how isolation and sensory deprivation affected behavior. Chimpanzees are highly social animals. They need interaction. I wasn't even allowed to look at them or talk to them. Just push a lever that dropped food into their cages." He stopped for a moment and stared out at the ocean.

When he started speaking again, his voice was thick with emotion. "One of the chimps wasn't eating, and I complained to my supervisor. He didn't do anything about it. I complained again and again, but they were just excited about finally having results they could measure. The chimp died. Of starvation. I was the one who found him, just a heap of skin and bones, his eyes glazed. I lost it. I stormed out of there and called a friend who introduced me to Barbara, the woman who started PETA. She's such an inspiration. . . ." His voice trailed off.

Pepe wriggled in my arms. "Did I ever tell you about how I refused to be in an experiment?" he asked.

"What happened?" I asked.

"We planned and carried off a perfect action. We liberated all those chimps, found them good homes, got on the news, started a swell of publicity and protests that ended in the department changing their policy on animal experimentation. It was a big story."

"I refused to allow them to plant some sort of monitoring equipment under my skin," said Pepe.

"Weren't there repercussions?" I asked.

"Yes, I was then shipped off like a prisoner with a bunch of other dogs," said Pepe, "though I had done nothing wrong."

"Well, I lost my job, got expelled from school, and went to jail."

"That's pretty serious."

"I know, but it brought me to you," said Pepe.

"Wait a minute," I said. "Are you talking about chipping?"

"What?" Ted was confused.

"I just wondered what you thought about chipping?" I asked, staring at Pepe. Had he really been able to avoid being chipped? Then maybe he was Caprice's dog, after all. Or maybe he avoided being chipped at the pound in Seattle.

"Oh, I think it's inhumane. Would we do that to people?" Ted said.

"But it's so the animals can be returned to their owners," I pointed out.

"Owner!" said Ted with a hoot of derision. "What a ridiculous name for the relationship between a human and an animal."

"You see, Geri," said Pepe, "I told you we do not use that term. We prefer *companion animal.*"

"Companion animal," I mused.

"Even that is a subservient relationship," Ted pointed out.

"I was thinking we were the companion animals," I said.

Ted didn't get it for a minute. Then he threw back his head and laughed. I liked it that he seemed able to feel everything so deeply: the pain of the monkeys, the beauty of the sunset, the humor of a comment. "Very good, Geri!" he said, squeezing me. "Have you ever thought of joining PETA? We're planning a big action tomorrow."

"Really? What?"

Just then, Ted's pocket began ringing. "Sorry!"

he said, reaching into it and pulling out his phone. He looked at the number. "I've got to get this." He got up and walked a short distance away. It was a brief conversation, consisting of "Yes," and "OK," and "Sure. I'll be there in a few minutes." He came back over to me. "I've got to go. Important meeting. I'm sorry. I'd love to spend more time with you. Maybe tomorrow?" He was already helping me to my feet. I brushed sand off my jeans.

"Tell him you will have your people call his people," said Pepe.

"I'll have my people check my schedule—" I began, then whirled around and faced Pepe, who was trotting behind us, doing his funny sand prance. "What are you talking about?"

"You have people?" Ted laughed.

"Yes, she has me," said Pepe.

"My dog is my social secretary," I explained.

"Well, if it's OK with him," said Ted, "I'd like to spend more time with you."

"She is busy," said Pepe.

"He says I'm busy," I said.

"Maybe if I bring him a treat," Ted said. "I know what dogs like."

"You do not know what I like!" Pepe was offended by the idea of being bribed. "Unless it is bacon."

"He likes bacon," I offered. We were back at the car, and Ted held the door open for me. Pepe jumped into my lap.

"No bacon," said Ted. "I can't sanction killing

anything that has a face. Do you know pigs are more intelligent than dogs?"

"I have changed my mind about him," said Pepe. "No way are you going out with a guy who thinks pigs are more intelligent than *perros*."

Chapter 15

Ted was suddenly in a rush to get rid of me. We raced back across town. There was just as much traffic this way, but he employed his shortcuts and soon we were pulling up in front of the hotel.

Ted stepped out of the car and handed his keys to the valet.

"No need to see me to my door," I said as I untangled myself from my seat belt.

"Oh, I wasn't intending to," he said. "My meeting is here at the hotel."

"Oh!"

He gave me a quick hug, then hurried away toward the pool area.

"What was that about?" I asked.

"Let us see who he meets, Geri," suggested Pepe, scurrying after him.

Although normally I would not condone such behavior, I had to follow my dog. Just in case there was a bigger dog at the pool that hassled him.

We followed a slate path that led past glossy green elephant ears and giant ferns and caught sight of Ted just as he was knocking on the door of Rebecca's bungalow. We ducked behind a potted palm, but Rebecca wasn't paying attention to us. She gave Ted the standard Hollywood greeting—a double kiss, one on each cheek— and then pulled him inside.

"Do not worry, Geri," said Pepe. "She cannot hold a candle to you in terms of beauty and youth. However, she does have *mucho dinero.*"

"Money isn't everything," I said, although it did seem to be the major motivator in L.A.

"What would Jimmy G do in this situation?" I wondered.

And Pepe answered, "He would investigate. And so will we." He ran at the door of the cottage, barking.

"But, Pepe," I said, rushing after him, "we can't just go barging in without some reason."

"We will come up with a story," said Pepe, "like the detectives do on TV."

"Like what?"

"We will say that I was pining away with *amor* for Siren Song and pulled you here against your will." He began barking and scratching at the door.

"Well, that is certainly true," I said.

"Remember, you must pretend surprise when you see Ted!" Pepe advised me as the door swung open. It was not Rebecca, but Luis,

Rebecca's hunky bodyguard and Siren Song's dance partner.

"Where's Rebecca?" I started, but then remembered our cover story. "Pepe wanted to play, and I thought I'd see if Siren Song was available. They play so well together."

"If only," said Pepe in a dreamy voice before hurrying past Luis and down the hall. I followed Pepe and Luis followed me.

"Rebecca's in a meeting," he said as we entered the living room, with its bank of windows overlooking a terrace. Rebecca was sitting in an armchair with a drink in her hand, and Ted was sitting across from her, his knees almost touching hers, leaning in, addressing her in passionate tones. He looked up, saw me, and broke off.

"Geri!" said Rebecca, turning her head and spotting me. "What are you doing here?"

"Pepe!" I said, holding out my hands as if to say, *What can you do with a dog like Pepe?* Of course, Pepe was nowhere around, so it didn't help my credibility.

"Well, this is a private conversation," Rebecca said. She looked at Ted, then back at me. "I have to meet with all of the choreographers every night to work out the plan for the next day's dances."

"I thought that was a decision made by the dance instructor working with the team," I said, trying to prolong the conversation.

"Don't be ridiculous!" Rebecca said, setting down her glass. "It's reality TV." She gave a short laugh, looked at Ted, and shook her head. She held up a thick sheaf of paper that had been lying in her lap and tapped it with her fingernail. "It's all scripted."

"Hollywood, baby," said Ted, leaning back in his chair. He seemed like an entirely different person. Gone was the earnest activist. Now his lip actually curled. Was he putting on an act for Rebecca? Or had he been putting on an act for me earlier?

Pepe came running into the room with Siren Song at his heels. I wanted him to hear what Rebecca had just told me.

"So it's not random?" I asked. "The assignments?"

Rebecca laughed. "No. We figure that all out ahead of time."

"How?" I asked.

"When the little dog comes into the room with the tags for you to choose your dance, all the tags have the same dance on them," she said. "We've already assigned it. We just change all the tags each time he enters a room."

"What else?" I asked. "The costumes? The dance routines? The judges' scores?"

"Well, obviously some of it we can't dictate," Rebecca said. "The accidents are sometimes the best bits."

"Like a fight between two dogs?" I asked, thinking of what Jake had told me.

"Hmmm," said Rebecca. "That's an interesting idea." She winked at Ted.

"Do you mean the whole show is fixed?" Pepe

asked. He was so indignant he had momentarily forgotten about Siren Song.

"I can't believe you would do that!" I said.

"Come on, Geri," said Ted. "It's reality TV. You don't think those shows are real, do you?"

"And this is just a pilot," said Rebecca. "We want to manage the results so the show has a real chance of being picked up."

"What about the winner?" I asked. "Do you already know who will win?"

Rebecca smiled, a strange, smug smile. "Actually we don't know that," she said. "We're still in negotiations."

"What do you mean negotiations?" I asked.

"Let's just say, money talks," Rebecca said. "Now run along." She snapped her fingers, and Siren Song ran over to her. Rebecca picked her up and put her on her lap. "I have business to conduct."

"What does she mean negotiating?" Pepe asked as Luis whisked us out the door.

"I'm not sure," I said, "but I think she meant that she might sell the win to whoever pays the most money."

"That is outrageous!" Pepe said as we headed up the stairs to our room. But by the time he had settled down on the pillow on top of the bed, he had changed his attitude. "Is there any way we can raise a large sum of money, Geri?"

I thought about that. Pepe knew I had spent most of the money we had earned on our last case catching up on my mortgage payments.

But if Pepe truly belonged to Caprice, and she gave me a reward for returning him to her, well, that would certainly be enough to make sure Pepe won *Dancing with Dogs.* I wondered. If it was a choice between fame or me, which would he choose?

Chapter 16

I went to call room service and noticed the red message light on my telephone. I picked it up, hoping it was Felix. But it was a message from my counselor, Susanna, calling from Seattle: "Geri, I'm worried about you. You promised to check in with me every day, and I haven't heard from you. I'll give you my cell phone number. Please call me as soon as you get this message!"

Oops! I had been so busy with the show and investigating, my life in Seattle seemed like a dream. I called the cell phone number, and Susanna answered on the second ring.

"Geri! How are you?"

"I'm fine," I said.

"I was so worried when I didn't hear from you." She sounded relieved.

"I've been a little distracted," I said.

"Why is that?"

"Well, did you hear about the murder?"

"What murder?" Her voice got sharp.

"Nigel St. Nigel."

"The mean judge from *So You Wanna Be a Star*? Yes, I heard about that. What does that have to do with you?"

"His body was found on our set. And, of course, because Pepe thinks he's a detective . . ."

"I *am* a detective," said Pepe, looking up from his show. "Do I not have a card with my name on it?"

"Yes, you do," I said. "So, anyway, Pepe insisted on investigating—"

"Is someone else in the room with you?"

"Just Pepe."

"There is no 'just' when speaking of Pepe," said Pepe.

"So you are talking to him?"

"Actually he's talking to me."

There was a long silence on the other end. I thought I should break it. I was eager to address my biggest concern. "He thinks he once belonged to Caprice Kennedy, the movie star."

"*Sí*, I am certain! "said Pepe.

"It sounds like you don't believe him."

"Well, he did find his way to her house, but"— I lowered my voice to a whisper—"there are some contraindications."

"I do understand that word," Pepe said in a cross voice. "And if you mean the fact that Caprice did not recognize me, that is sad but true. Luckily she seems to be coming around." He stuck out his pink tongue and licked his nose, a gesture of satisfaction. Or maybe he was just looking for crumbs left over from his dinner.

Didn't he understand how his comments about Caprice made me feel?

"Naturally I'm terrified. What if she reclaims him?"

Pepe looked at me thoughtfully, then came over and sat in my lap.

"So you are worried that your dog will leave you to live with a movie star?" Susanna asked.

"Yes," I said.

"You would be abandoned again. Like when your parents died. And your ex-husband left you."

"That's true." I was thoughtful.

"I know that's painful to contemplate."

I thought about that. Was it true? That I was getting my dog mixed up with past sorrows?

Susanna spoke up. "Geri, is there any way I can talk you into returning to Seattle? I think you have more support systems there."

"No, we're doing really well in the competition. Pepe would never leave until he wins *Dancing with Dogs*."

"Until *we* win!" said Pepe, giving me some credit.

Our dance for the third day of the competition was a salsa, a dance that Pepe took to as if it had been bred into him. Our choreographer was Sofia, a sexy Latina with long brunette hair that she liked to toss around and a voluptuous body that she poured into a tight spandex jumpsuit. She adored Pepe and he adored her.

He sauntered back and forth on his hind legs, wiggling his little hips left and right.

I had a much more difficult time. My hips didn't seem to move much at all, and apparently I was bouncing up when I was supposed to be getting down. "Think of the floor as your enemy. You are grinding him beneath your heel," said Sofia. The music was fast and infectious. A cheerful blend of horns and strings that could drive a truck right through a brick wall. The routine involved much circling around and advancing forward and backing up for me and Pepe.

About halfway through the rehearsal, I heard a lot of barking and growling. We dashed down the hall and saw a group of people gathered around the doorway of one of the rooms. Inside, Max, the poodle, was snarling and snapping at the German shepherd. Ted was in the room, trying to pull the German shepherd away by the hindquarters. He was shouting at the other people in the room, giving them instructions, but everyone was standing around frozen. And the poodle kept rushing at the shepherd, jaws snapping, teeth slashing.

Jake, the Certified Animal Safety Representative, rushed in behind me. He saw Ted and stopped for a moment, startled, but then he grabbed the hind legs of the poodle.

"Good work!" he said to Ted. "Now circle him so he can't bite you." They both began to walk their dogs around like wheelbarrows in big circles. The dogs kept turning their heads to snap at each other, but they couldn't reach the other dog.

"Whose dog is supposed to be in this room?" Jake asked.

"It's the shepherd's room," said Ted. "We were working on a routine when the poodle came dashing in." He looked over at Rebecca, who was standing on the edge of the crowd next to Maxine, the poodle's owner. Neither one of them seemed too concerned.

"OK." Jake edged the poodle toward the door. "Everybody out," he said. "Let the dogs calm down. I'll call the vet to come and check out both dogs."

In a few minutes, the fight was over and the crowd slowly dispersed. I saw Rebecca go over and talk to Ted. Had they set up the fight to have some good footage for the show? It seemed the opposite of what Ted would want. But then again he would have film to show that the dogs were being harmed during the production of the show.

As soon as we arrived at the soundstage, we ran into Alice, the vet.

"I forgot my scanner," she said. "But I could check your dog to see if he has a chip."

"I don't know if this is a good time," I said. I didn't really want to discuss chips in front of Pepe, so I tried to hurry him along.

"It is always a good time for chips," said Pepe, slowing down and looking up at her. "I love chips, especially Cheetos."

"I should be able to tell if he has one," Alice said, picking him up and running her fingers along his back. She paused, digging her fingers into the folds of loose fur around his neck.

"*¡Sí!* That is the spot!" said Pepe. "It has always been bumpy."

Alice looked thoughtful. "Definitely chipped!" she said. "Do you want to feel it?"

"When is she going to give us the chips?" Pepe asked.

"We'll go get them right now," I said, taking Pepe away from Alice. "Thank you!" I said.

"I'll bring my scanner tomorrow," she said.

"We do not need a scanner for the chips like in the supermarket," said Pepe. "They have free chips for the taking right here on the craft service table."

I got Pepe some Cheetos before heading for the costume room. I'd been worried about the costumes for the salsa since they tended to be scanty for the Latin dances. I was right to be worried. While Pepe looked adorable in a glittery vest, my dress was merely a bunch of sequins sewn onto a flesh-colored net. Even worse, I was supposed to wear it with four-inch-high gold heels.

I almost stumbled going down the stairs, and although I managed to regain my composure and get through the number, I was not impressed by our performance. I was shaken by the thought that Pepe really was chipped. And Pepe was off as well. He seemed to be distracted by something that was happening offstage.

Our scores turned out to reflect my opinion. Beverly gave us an eight ("for teamwork"), Miranda gave us a seven ("for good partnering"), and Caprice gave us a six. Pepe was crushed. For the first time, we were in the bottom two and had to stand onstage while the camera zoomed in on our faces. I was trying not to cry. And I could feel Pepe trembling in my arms.

But it was the German shepherd who got sent home. I bet Ted was disappointed. It was the first time a routine he had choreographed—in this case, a disco number—got the lowest scores.

After the performance, there was always a bit of a letdown. We had to go back to makeup and costumes and get everything undone. I always felt more comfortable when I was back in my jeans and a cotton blouse. But Pepe and I were both dejected by our brush with failure. I realized that I was just as invested as Pepe in winning.

We were leaving makeup and heading for the door when Jimmy G came rushing up, yelling, "It's gotta be here! It's gotta be here!"

"What?" I asked.

"The package!" he yelled, clutching at his tie as if it were strangling him. "It wasn't at Klamp's house, so it's got to be here!"

"You went to Rodney's house?"

"What did Jimmy G just say?"

"And he wasn't there?"

"What? Are you an echo?"

"I guess he wasn't there," said Pepe.

"Only the damned police," said Jimmy G. "And they wanted to know why Jimmy G was on the scene. Seemed to think Klamp might be in some kind of trouble and had the nerve to accuse Jimmy G of gunning for him. Jimmy G will gun for him, for sure, if he made off with my package!" His face was a fiery red, especially his nose. "They took Jimmy G down to the police station and grilled Jimmy G all night. Jimmy G just got out in time for your performance." He turned and gave me a wink. "Wouldn't have missed that for anything! You dress up nice, doll!"

"Thanks."

"Jimmy G did get a chance to look around before the coppers showed up. No package anywhere. So either that Klamp made off with it, or it's still here somewhere."

He looked around. Most of the lights were off, creating dark shadows around the edges of the soundstage.

"Where did you last see the package?" Jimmy G asked. "It was back here somewhere, right?"

"Over there," I said, pointing to the greenroom. "I set it down in the greenroom. I asked Rodney to put it someplace safe. If Rodney picked it up and moved it, he could have put it anywhere."

Jimmy G scoured the greenroom, then headed for the area behind it, which also happened to be the place where the techs piled all of the equipment that was either broken or not in use. There were canvases and ladders, coils of wire, and banks of lights. Jimmy G dove into the pile and started pushing things around, making a terrible clatter.

"Stop it! You'll get us in trouble!" I looked around, sure that someone would come running thanks to all the noise Jimmy G was making. But then it got worse.

"Good God Almighty!" Jimmy G shrieked. He had thrown back a canvas, and now he stared down at the object he had uncovered. He looked at me, his face a pale moon in the dim light of the corner. I heard footsteps running toward us.

"What is it?" I said. "Did you find the package?"

"No, he did not," said Pepe.

"No, Jimmy G found a body!"

Chapter 17

"Step away, Geri!" said Pepe. He tried to nudge me backward. He had already run forward to inspect Jimmy G's find, then back to me.

I ignored him. Hadn't I already seen two dead bodies during our last case? I considered myself hardened. But I wasn't prepared for what I saw when I finally inched forward, with Pepe tucked firmly under my arm.

It was Jake, the Certified Animal Safety Representative, sprawled on the floor. His face was purple, his eyes bulging, his tongue protruding. A choke chain was wrapped around his neck. I turned away, sickened.

About the same time, a few other crew members arrived on the scene, responding to Jimmy G's strangled shriek. Someone dialed 911. Someone went to get Rebecca. No one tried to resuscitate Jake, not even the EMTs when they arrived. It was quite clear to everyone that he was dead.

"Who was that guy?" Jimmy G asked as he sat

on a chair, his hands on his belly, trying to calm his heaving stomach.

"Jake. I don't know his last name. He is, he *was*, the Certified Animal Safety Representative," I said.

"Do you think he found Jimmy G's package?" he asked.

"Wow! There must be something really valuable in that package," I said, "if you think people are getting murdered for it."

Jimmy G put his forefinger up against his lips. "Keep it on the hush-hush, babe. Jimmy G didn't mention the package to the police. Not good for them to know Jimmy G's business."

"Don't you think that's a mistake?" I said.

"Private dicks and the police don't mix," said Jimmy G. "Like cats and dogs. Always been that way. Always will be."

The same detectives who investigated Nigel's murder came back for this homicide: Sam Scott, the tall blond Nordic type, and his partner who looked like Kyra Sedgwick. This time, she was wearing a gray pencil skirt and a navy polka-dot blouse with a navy blue cardigan and a pencil tucked into her French twist.

Scott took charge of the crime scene and ordered everyone back, but people still milled around the edges of the yellow crime scene tape that had been strung up by one of the uniformed LAPD patrolmen who was first on the scene.

"Why would anybody want to kill an hombre

who cared so much about the welfare of us *perros?*" asked Pepe.

Rebecca, who had been pacing back and forth, provided a possible answer to Pepe's question. "Somebody's trying to sabotage my show!"

"What makes you say that?" Scott asked, slipping underneath the crime scene tape and coming up to her, small notepad in hand.

"*Dos muertos,*" said Pepe, "could easily equal sabotage."

"Isn't it obvious?" Rebecca told Scott. "What else could it be? First, Nigel St. Nigel and now Jake."

"That is what I was saying," said Pepe.

"Can you keep your dog quiet?" Scott told me. It was more of an order than a question.

"Shhhh!" I told my pooch. "You need to stop kibitzing."

He looked up at me. "I fail to understand what an Israeli collective has to do with anything."

"That's a *kibbutz,*" I told him. "Now be quiet. Do you want us to get kicked out of here?"

"I was only observing," said Pepe. "Is that not what we private detectives do?"

"That's it!" shouted Scott, turning on me and Pepe. "Get back!"

"Fine by me," said Pepe. "The smell of *los muertos* disagrees with my appetite—and it *is* getting on to dinnertime."

"But nobody leaves," the detective said. "I'll want to question each of you individually."

* * *

The uniformed police separated us and told us not to talk to each other. There weren't many of us: me and Pepe and Jimmy G and Robyn from the costume shop. Two of the cameramen were also present, as were one of the grips and Rebecca. She was furious. Or else she concealed her fear beneath anger. She paced back and forth, muttering loudly to herself.

Just then there was a commotion at the door.

"I tell you, I have important information for the police!" It was the screechy voice of Miranda Skarbos. She pushed her way past the policeman on duty and stormed down the aisle. She was dressed in her usual gypsy Bohemian getup: a full black skirt with a ragged edge, a glittery sequined top, and a tight black satin jacket. A long red scarf was looped around her neck many times. Her wild, bushy gray hair streamed behind her. As she waved her bony hands in the air, the fringe on her scarf quivered.

Scott frowned. He motioned to one of the policemen who tried to stop Miranda, but she breezed right by him and headed for the scene of the crime.

"Who is this?" asked Scott.

"She's an animal psychic," I said. "She's one of the judges on the show."

"It happened here!" She strode dramatically over to the area where Jimmy G had found Jake's body.

"Of course she knows where he was found," said Pepe. "It is obvious from the yellow crime scene tape."

"Since when did you become a skeptic?" I asked.

"Since she gave us such a low score for our salsa," Pepe replied.

"Ma'am, stay back behind the tape," Scott said.

"I received a message telling me I needed to return. There is a traumatized spirit here, calling out to me." Miranda looked around, her gray frizzled hair flying. "I can see the fear she felt, the loud voices, the frenzy of the killer, the heated words, angry words!"

The two detectives looked at each other and rolled their eyes.

"Ma'am, the victim is a man!" said Scott.

"I'm not talking about him!" Miranda dismissed the corpse with a wave of her hand. "I'm talking about the dog. She was scared. This man came to her rescue. And then she had to watch as her persecutor choked him to death."

"Dog? There were no dogs in the vicinity, were there?" Scott asked.

Everyone looked around. But Pepe was the only dog in sight.

"He's been with me all night," I said.

"This is a female dog," said Miranda, closing her eyes and swaying back and forth. "A small dog. A precious little soul, a furry little love bomb."

"Siren Song!" said Pepe with a sigh. Then he began to wriggle in my arms. "Put me down, Geri!" he commanded.

I did as he asked, and he dashed over to the

crime scene, where he began sniffing around, his head moving back and forth.

"Get that dog out of here!" Scott said. "He's contaminating the crime scene."

"Pepe, come!" I said, but my command sounded feeble, and Pepe ignored me. I tried again, "Pepe, come!" then remembered what Felix had taught me in the one training session I had: "Never deliver the same command twice. Wait until he performs the command, then reward him."

I waited but still he did not respond. Finally, as one of the detectives was about to scoop him up, he came running back to me.

"It *was* Siren Song," he said. "She was frightened, as this woman says. We must find her!"

Miranda was going on. "She is surrounded by darkness. She is confused, unable to move. She's so frightened. She is begging us to rescue her."

"I will rescue you, Siren Song," Pepe declared.

"Could it be Siren Song?" I asked Rebecca.

She looked worried. "She should be with Luis," she said. She pulled out her cell phone and hit one button. Evidently, Luis answered quickly. There was a long pause; then Rebecca frowned. "You've got to be kidding me. Right?" Another pause. "Ridiculous!" she snapped. "I'll deal with this later!" Then she clicked her phone shut and turned to Scott. "My dog is back at the hotel room and she's fine. In fact, she's sleeping. My assistant just went and checked on her."

"Get this woman out of here!" Scott commanded, gesturing at Miranda.

I felt sorry for her as she was hustled away, protesting that she had been sent to deliver a message from this troubled dog.

The police took me and Pepe and Jimmy G to Parker Center to ask us more questions, since we had been the ones to find the body. I didn't have much to add. When they asked me if I knew anyone who would want to harm Jake, Pepe suggested I tell them about the confrontation between Ted and Jake, but I didn't want to say anything until I had a chance to talk to Ted.

Pepe wanted to rush back to the hotel and check on Siren Song as soon as we were released, but Jimmy G was hungry and insisted on getting something to eat. I agreed. Even Pepe was persuaded when Jimmy G mentioned Pink's.

"I have been there many times with Caprice," he said. "Usually late at night after some serious partying. It is one of the best places in L.A. to see and be seen."

Chapter 18

Pink's looked just like any other hot dog stand, except for the long lines of people standing outside, people of all sizes, shapes, ages, and races. Young women in skimpy sequin dresses and high heels giggling as they tried to cram the foot-long dogs into their mouths. And also some guys on Harleys with gray beards and leather jackets.

Jimmy G was impressed. While I read down the menu trying to find something without meat, he saw some guy walking away with what looked like a chili dog on steroids. It must have weighed a couple of pounds and was piled high with everything from guacamole and sour cream to heaps of shredded cheddar, onions, and fresh salsa.

"That's for me!" said Jimmy G.

I finally ordered a vegan dog I found at the bottom of the menu. Pepe wanted a plain hot dog and bun. "I am a purist," he said. "And when speaking to me, please refer to it as a frankfurter, *por favor*. I do not eat *dogs*, hot or otherwise."

We got our food and found a seat at one of the many picnic tables set up around the place. I offered to cut up Pepe's frankfurter for him, but he declined, saying, "*Gracias*, but I have sharp teeth. Besides, I like to hear it squeak when I bite into it."

"So," I asked my boss as he shoveled huge mouthfuls of chili dog into his face, "what happened? You were at Rodney's house and ran into the police?"

"They ran into Jimmy G is more like it," he said, a stray chili bean rolling down his chin and back onto his plate. "Damned cops! Barely got into the house and found the place trashed, like somebody had torn it all up searching for something. Which is what Jimmy G was doing, but, of course, no Rodney or my package anywhere to be found."

"Somebody had tossed the *casa*?" asked Pepe.

"The house had been ransacked?" I asked.

"Yeah," said Jimmy G. "Then in come the flatfeet like gangbusters, and it's 'Freeze!' and 'Hands up!' and 'On your knees!' and they're slapping on the handcuffs and trying to make Jimmy G's face part of the carpet."

"Gee," I said.

"Gee isn't the half of it," said my boss.

"They must have thought you were a burglar, huh?" I asked. "So what happened?"

"They took Jimmy G down to the station and grilled him, like he said. Hours and hours but they never broke your boss. Told them Jimmy G was a PI working a case. Went to that particular address. Found the gate open and the front door open and went in to look around. What could they say?" He took another big bite of his chili dog and chewed it thoughtfully. "No evidence to link Jimmy G to any crime."

"So they let you go."

"They said Jimmy G is a person of interest and shouldn't leave town," he said. "They also said that Washington private eyes don't have reprisossity . . ." He stopped and tried again. "Recipe-osse?"

"You mean reciprocity?"

"Something like that. Anyway it means Jimmy G can't investigate while here." He wolfed down the last of his chili dog and added, "Something fishy going on with all this, that's all Jimmy G knows."

"Did the cops have any information about Rodney?" I asked.

"Nope," he said. "That's what had them worried. Guy disappeared. No sign of him. Did he clean out the place and make off with a bunch of items that didn't belong to him? Or was he the victim of a crime?"

"Still," said Pepe, "it is very hinky."

"*Hinky*, huh?" I said to my dog. "When did you ever start using a word like *hinky*?"

"Since we have been working with our boss, Jimmy G," he told me matter-of-factly. "Is the word not appropriate to the situation?"

I couldn't deny that the word fit, so I asked Jimmy G, "What are you going to do now?"

"Going to find Jimmy G's damn package," he said. "That's what!"

"And that won't be a problem?"

"Not really. Jimmy G's not working for a client. Just following up on a package sent to Jimmy G himself. The Jimmy G Detective Agency is not involved in anything else—officially, at least."

"The Jimmy G Detective Agency?" I asked. "I thought we were the Gerrard Detective Agency."

"Decided to change the name," said my boss. "Put the main attraction front and center, which is *me,* Jimmy G." He gave me a quizzical look. "Didn't Jimmy G tell you?"

"No, actually you didn't."

"Well, consider yourself told. That reminds me." He reached into his jacket's inner pocket and pulled out a rubber-banded stack of business cards. "New business cards. Designed them myself."

I pulled one of the cards out and looked it over. It had THE JIMMY G DETECTIVE AGENCY across the top in bold, red letters. Then, in smaller letters, it read JIMMY GERRARD, PRIVATE INVESTIGATOR.

"Let me see," Pepe told me. I pulled him up into my lap so he could look at the card. "Holy guacamole!" he said. "I like the smoking *pistola* on this new card."

A smoking pistol was indeed incorporated into the design. Printed beside it was what I took for our new motto: WE ALWAYS FIND THE SMOKING GUN!

"Clever, huh?" said Jimmy G with an ear-to-ear grin. "Jimmy G wrote the slogan himself."

"Ask him, what if there is no gun used in a crime we are investigating?" said Pepe. "Would not this smoking gun logo then be inappropriate?"

I relayed Pepe's concern to my boss. He looked hurt.

"Hey," he said, "the smoking gun thing is just a metaphor. Or a simile. Hell, I can never tell those two apart. Anyhow, take a gander at the other names on the card."

I smiled when I saw my name: GERI SULLIVAN, ASSOCIATE. And right below that was PEPE SULLIVAN, ASSOCIATE.

"You put Pepe's name on the card?"

"Do not complain, Geri," Pepe told me. "I like it!"

"Jimmy G put your dog's name on it so it looks like we've got more troops in the field. The more the better when it comes to getting new clients."

"I see," I told him. "So Pepe and I are *associates*?"

"Yeah. You like that word, *associate*? Pretty classy, huh?"

I started to open my mouth to say that I'd rather have the term *private investigator* after my name, but Pepe stopped me short, saying, "Geri, do not complain. It is much better than Gal Friday, is it not?"

I thought a moment, then said, "Yes," which Jimmy G took for an answer to his own question.

"Copacetic," said my boss. "Now it's time to get to work." He got up from the table, straightened out his sport coat, and slapped his hands together. "Jimmy G is going on the hunt for that package! I need to know everything you know about the package."

I described it to him again. The shape, the

duct tape, the weight, the way the address was written with a felt-tip pen on the brown wrapping paper.

"And you didn't see who delivered it?"

I shook my head. "But you must have an idea or you wouldn't have come down here," I said.

"It's got to be Nacho," he said, shaking his head.

"Nacho?"

"I told you, Geri," said Pepe.

"Guy Jimmy G knew in the first Gulf War. We called him Nacho because he was always eating Nacho Cheese Doritos."

"And you think he sent this package to you?" I asked. "What's in it?"

"Jimmy G cannot tell you that. Classified information."

"Oh," I said. "Well, why don't you just call this guy up and talk to him?"

"Jimmy G cannot do that. Jimmy G and Nacho had a falling out a few years ago."

"Really? Why?"

"Again, Jimmy G cannot reveal that. Unsavory. Not a story for the ladies. But Jimmy G lost touch with Nacho as a result."

"Well, you are a PI, aren't you?"

Jimmy G nodded.

"So find him!"

Jimmy G laughed. One thing I could say about my boss, he was always good-tempered.

"You're right, doll! Jimmy G will go looking for Nacho! Most logical thing in the world. Don't know why Jimmy G didn't think of it."

Chapter 19

Pepe and I took a taxi back to the hotel, while Jimmy G set off to find Nacho. As soon as we got out of the car, Pepe said, "I must talk to Siren Song. I am *muy* worried over the evil, dark foreboding sensed by the pet psychic."

"You were fine at dinner."

"Food is one thing—worry is another. It is best never to mix them," he said. "I have finished eating, and I am now worried."

"Rebecca said Siren Song was fine."

"I must see her with my own eyes to be satisfied of that."

"But—"

"Geri," he interrupted. "If you love me, you will take me to her."

Of course we went to the cottage. Even before we got to the door, we could hear angry voices inside. One definitely belonged to Rebecca. No one responded to my knock. So I tried again. Still no response.

"Allow me," said Pepe, and he began scratching at the door and yipping and whining. To my surprise, this worked.

Rebecca flung open the door. She clearly hadn't expected to see me and Pepe. "What do you want?"

"We wanted to check on Siren Song," I said, although that sounded lame, even to me. Pepe went rushing past Rebecca and into the cottage. I could see Luis. He was sitting on the sofa in the living room. He looked dejected, whereas Rebecca just looked angry. Her face was flushed.

"We're not in the mood for visitors," Rebecca said. "It's been a very upsetting day. The management company is threatening to end the shoot. Just because there have been two murders on the set. How is that my fault?"

"Yes, what could you do about that?" I agreed.

"Something about insurance," Rebecca went on. "And the police are no better. I told them that unless the set is released by one p.m. tomorrow, I'm going elsewhere. Not that there's anyplace else we could go on such short notice."

"I'm sorry," I said. "I'll just get Pepe and we'll leave." I tried to edge around Rebecca, who was blocking the door. But just then, Pepe came running back.

"The door to the bedroom is closed. But I cannot smell Siren Song," he said. He was shaking as only an upset Chihuahua can shake.

"Are you sure she's OK?" I asked Rebecca.

"She's resting. She had a hard day. Your dog

should not have outperformed her. It was demoralizing for her."

"I'll talk to him about that," I said. But I didn't.

When we got back to the room, Pepe was still worried about Siren Song, but he got distracted by one of his favorite telenovellas: *Paraiso perdido*. I turned on my laptop so I could check my e-mail. I didn't really expect anything. My sister didn't know I was out of town. She would have just lectured me, big sister style, if she found out I was flying to L.A. to appear in a reality TV show. My best friend, Brad, prefers to communicate via Facebook, so I logged into my Facebook account to check on him. To my surprise, a friend request popped up from Pepe Sullivan.

"Pepe, have you been messing with my computer?"

"Do you not want to be my friend?" he asked.

"Pepe!" I didn't know what to say. "How did you—"

"You were asleep. I was bored." He seemed quite happy with himself. "The keyboard is just the right size for my paws." He held up one of his delicate little feet. "The mouse, however, was truculent." He glared at it as if it really were a mouse. "I would like to snap its little spine in my sharp teeth." He snapped his teeth and shook his head back and forth.

"No! Do not do that!" I said, covering the

black plastic mouse with my cupped hands. "You are not allowed to use my laptop, Pepe!"

"Then how will I respond to my many friends?" he asked. I looked at his profile page. Employed by Sullivan and Sullivan Detective Agency. Attended Dog Obedience School (nine times). Lives in Seattle. And he had 191 friends. How is that possible? I have only 58 (mostly classmates from college and high school). I felt a pang of jealousy. Especially when I saw that he was friends with Caprice.

"In addition, I can help you do research!" Pepe said. "I saw that you were looking at pictures of me and Caprice."

I felt a pang of guilt. Did he know how much he was worth to Caprice?

"I am surprised you did not look for Nigel and his dog."

"I was just about to do that," I said. Nothing worse than being scolded by your dog.

"Let me know when you find something," Pepe said, and turned back to the TV. The commercial was over and Corinna was back in the arms of the handsome UPS deliveryman. Little did she know that Hector was watching through the window.

I typed in the words *Nigel St. Nigel* and *dog* and immediately got a million hits and fifty photos. Apparently Nigel's dog was famous. She was a Chinese crested, one of those strange dogs that looks a bit like a shaved rat with a pompadour. In fact, she had won the title of the Ugliest Dog in the World a few years back.

Pepe drew back with a start when I showed

him the photo of the snaggletoothed beast with the crossed eyes and strange saggy gray skin.

"*¡Ay ay ay!!*" he said. "What is that?"

"A dog," I replied. "The Ugliest Dog in the World, to be exact."

"If that is a dog, then it indeed deserves that title," said Pepe.

"And it's Nigel St. Nigel's dog."

"Really?" Pepe studied it intently. "I am surprised that such a creature smells just like a dog but a dog it must be."

"Poor thing!" I said, looking at its floppy pouf of hair that flapped over its crossed eyes. "I wonder what happened to it."

"Her," said Pepe. "The dog I smelled was female."

"You are right!" I said, studying the caption. "Her name is Kooky. I wonder if she ran off after Nigel was killed?"

"No, the scent was older than that," said Pepe. "She had been gone for at least two days before Nigel was killed."

"Perhaps she was in the house," I pointed out. "Or at the vet. Or in a kennel."

Pepe shook his head. "I think there is perhaps a connection between her disappearance and Nigel's murder," said Pepe.

"You think that because you think dogs are so valuable," I began, then stopped, remembering the price on Pepe's head.

"You must admit this dog is valuable," said Pepe. "The Ugliest Dog in the World is not a title I would want, but it is a title, after all."

"You have to wonder why Nigel wanted her,"

I said. I clicked on one of the news stories about the contest and read about how Nigel had offered the owner of the dog over six figures for Kooky. The speculation was that he took a wicked pleasure in flaunting his ugly dog in a Hollywood culture that valued beauty. He was photographed everywhere with her, letting her lick his ears, cuddling with her in a chair, carrying her tucked in his arm at premieres. Or maybe he had been just as crazy in love with her as I am with Pepe.

Chapter 20

The phone barely began to ring in the morning, when Pepe knocked the receiver to the floor. He hopped down from the bed and spoke into it. "*¿Bueno? Sí, gracias,* we are awake." Then he hopped back up on the bed and began licking my face. "That was our wake-up call, Geri."

"Great," I said, reaching down and fumbling for the receiver. That reminded me that my cell phone was still missing. I wondered where it was. And where was Rodney?

"Rise and shine, partner!" Pepe exhorted me. "It is breakfast time! A big bowl of beef stew would hit the spot."

"Oh, God . . . ," I muttered, putting the phone back together.

"On second thought," Pepe told me. "I would prefer crispy corned beef hash with eggs from room service. And a side of bacon—also crispy, not limp!"

I dragged myself up to a sitting position and

leaned against the headboard. "Slow down. I'm still half asleep."

"A good breakfast will cure all ills," he told me. "*¡Andale!* Call room service."

I picked up the phone, saying, "Well, you don't seem to be worried about a thing anymore, do you?"

"What?" Pepe asked, scratching behind his ear with a hind leg. "You mean about Siren Song?"

"Yes," I said, trying to rub the sleep out of my eyes.

"I could worry about her," he told me, "but I am also hungry. Let me share with you a pearl of wisdom that I learned from a wise old dog high atop a mountain in the Sierra Madre: 'Worry does not produce food. But eating can ease worry. Ergo: if in doubt, always eat.' That is the *perro's* mantra."

I didn't want to hurt his feelings by telling him it sounded like a false syllogism. Instead, I just said, "Fine. I'll call room service. It's probably better to eat now than later. We wouldn't want to be dancing on a full stomach."

"I beg to differ," said Pepe.

"What do you mean?"

"It is always better to do *anything* on a full stomach."

I called room service, then dragged myself out of bed and headed for the shower. I hadn't gone ten feet when Pepe rushed past me and started jumping up and down at the door to our room.

"Take me outside, *pronto!*" he yelled. "I need to pee!" It was one of the hassles of having a dog. I pulled on a pair of sweats and sandals and tiptoed down the stairs with Pepe.

Pepe took his time, watering various plants that lined the pool. Luckily no one was poolside at 7:30 in the morning. It was a lovely day. The sky was blue and cloudless. If only my own life were so trouble-free.

Just as Pepe was finishing up, I saw Rebecca and Luis leaving the bungalow with a strange woman with a big bouffant hairdo. She was carrying a plastic dog kennel. I wondered who she was. Perhaps a new choreographer. Perhaps they had been rehearsing during the night, giving Siren Song an unfair advantage for tonight's performance. I couldn't really object. It was Rebecca's show, and if she wanted her dog to win, well, her dog could win. It would upset Pepe, but since he loved Siren Song, he couldn't be too upset.

Despite his hearty breakfast, Pepe practically danced up the steps to the rehearsal studio. I noticed there were more cameramen and lighting techs around than usual. Rebecca must be up to something new.

I followed behind more slowly. It turned out that Pepe had an ulterior motive. He went racing down the hallway and dashed into the open door of one of the rehearsal rooms. From within came the sound of snarling and yapping, and a second later, Pepe came running back out.

"Something is wrong!" he said. "Siren Song does not smell right!" He was shaking.

I looked into the room and saw Luis and Rebecca and the strange blond woman with the bouffant hair. Siren Song had run up to them, but when she saw Pepe in the doorway, she started back toward him, growling.

"What did you do?" I asked, picking him up and checking him for injuries. He seemed fine.

"*Nada,*" he said. "I just sniffed her butt and told her that she smelled funny and she attacked me!"

"Yes, women don't like that," I said with a chuckle.

"What's wrong with your dog?" Rebecca asked.

"He thinks there's something wrong with your dog. She smells funny." I could even smell it: a faint odor of ammonia and perfume.

"She just had a beauty treatment, that's all!" said Rebecca. "Your dog could probably use some extra grooming."

Pepe shook his head expressively and sneezed. I knew Pepe did not like perfume. Perhaps he was reacting to whatever product they had used on Siren Song.

"Is your dog getting sick?" Rebecca asked. "Get him away from here and make sure the vet checks him out today." She shooed us out of the room.

"I am not sick," said Pepe. "Just sick of lies!" He said it with all the drama of any telenovella actor.

"You better get moving. You're definitely going to need all the time you can get." Rebecca practically pushed us down the hall and into a room. To my surprise, Ted was in there, setting up the music. He wore tailored black pants and a simple white linen shirt, open at the neck. Usually he just wore sweats and a T-shirt.

"You look good!" I said. "But aren't you a little overdressed?"

"Got to look good for the waltz," he said.

"Where's the little dog with the tags to tell us what dance to do?" I asked, looking around.

"Oh, they'll film that bit later. We've got a lot to cover today. We should get started!"

I thought I knew a little bit about the waltz, as I remembered watching my parents waltz around the living room. But it turned out to be more complicated than I thought.

We practiced without music; we practiced with music. Since Pepe and I could not dance together because of our height differential, Ted had us practice separately. Pepe got the rhythm right away and could turn in perfect little circles in a big circle around the room.

About halfway through, a cameraman and a gaffer entered the room. They always liked to film a bit of the rehearsal.

"It's going to be tricky to make this look like a waltz," Ted said, "because waltzing is all about dancing together. But maybe"—he got a mischievous gleam in his eye—"we'll make this a story about a young woman who dances around her living room alone, imagining her perfect partner, never noticing her small dog who is dancing in perfect unison with her until she recognizes her true love has been in front of her all along."

Pepe sighed. "So *romántico*! A story worthy of a telenovela."

"I suppose," I said, trying to sound enthusiastic, but I didn't like the implication that I couldn't find a man.

"So let's have you practice turning in circles with your eyes closed," Ted said, "with your arms held out to your imaginary partner."

"What if I run into something? Or step on Pepe?"

"Believe me, I will stay out of your way, Geri," said Pepe. "My eyes will not be closed."

"I'll let you know if you are going to run into something," Ted said. There was just a hint of amusement in his voice.

He turned on the music, a contemporary waltz, and set me up at one end of the room. "Now dance in circles to your left," he said.

I felt really silly, especially since the camera was filming me, but I held out my arms and began turning, concentrating on the rhythm.

"Remember! Dreamy smile!" said Ted.

I lifted my face up toward the ceiling and imagined a perfect partner. And suddenly he was there. I felt hands touching mine, then a hand around my waist, a hand holding mine. For a moment we were moving at odds with each other as I fought to keep my pattern; then I surrendered to the sureness and solidity of my partner and was swept away into the dance. It was breathtaking!

"Ted?" I breathed, opening my eyes.

And got the shock of my life! It was Felix! My quasi-boyfriend from Seattle. He was smiling at me. He looked good. His teeth were white against the caramel color of his skin. His dark hair was a bit rumpled. His brown eyes sparkled.

I prayed he hadn't heard me call him Ted. But the camera probably did. Ted stood to one side, his arms folded, with a rather tight-lipped smile on his face. There were two cameras in the room now. One was filming me and Felix. The other guy was moving, taking in the expressions of the others in the room. Pepe was over in the corner, ignored, and I could see that annoyed him. Rebecca was standing in the doorway watching.

"What are you doing here?" I gasped.

"Happy to see me?" Felix asked.

"Of course, but surprised!"

He nodded his head toward the door. "The producers arranged to fly me down, as a prize, I guess you would say, for doing so well in the competition."

"Oh!" I clung to him. "I'm so glad to see you." Still it was weird. Our relationship was so new I didn't know how to treat him. A long lingering kiss was what I wanted, but the whole thing was a setup, and I felt used.

"How did you get the time off work?" And then I got it. His being so evasive. His working so many hours. "You did that for me?"

"Well, of course. I had to be here to support my best girl."

Hmm . . . That was an ambiguous term. Not "my girlfriend." Not "my sweetheart." "Best girl."

"And her dog," he went on.

"Rehearsal's over!" said Rebecca, clapping her hands. The cameramen took another couple of staged shots. They took shots of the little white dog trotting in and me taking the tag off his neck and miming surprise at the news we would be learning the waltz. They took shots of Felix talking about his work in Seattle and how we met. They took shots of me sitting and talking to Felix with Pepe on my lap.

Then they left. Ted was packing up during the filming. He had been silent the whole time. I felt a little guilty flirting with Felix in front of him.

"What about the waltz?" I said as he headed out of the room. "We didn't finish the rehearsal."

"Yeah, that's too bad," said Ted. "But that's the way Rebecca wanted it!"

"You mean she screwed up our rehearsal? She wants us to lose tonight?" I was suddenly on my feet, indignant.

Ted shrugged. "It was all a setup so she could get a good surprise shot when your boyfriend showed up."

"But we still have to have a routine for tonight!"

"You'll figure something out," he said, and left the room.

Pepe ran after him growling and barking. "It is sabotage, Geri!" he said.

"I know!" I stood there looking at the empty door.

"So who is that guy, Geri?" Felix asked. "He seems like a bit of a jerk."

"He is a jerk," I said. "He's supposed to be our choreographer, but he's really just working undercover for PETA."

"Why has no one kicked him out?" Felix asked.

"That's a good question," I said. "I think Rebecca knows who he is. But I believe he's planning some kind of action that will get publicity for PETA. And Rebecca loves publicity. She says there's no such thing as bad publicity. I can't believe he just left us without finishing the choreography."

"Well, I would try to help you," said Felix. "I know the waltz. But I have to get over to the soundstage. I have a job."

"You have a job? I thought you came to see me."

"Yes, but Rebecca wanted to kill two birds with one stone. She hired me to take the place of the guy who was killed, the Certified Animal Safety Representative."

"You can do that?"

"Yes, I was certified years ago. I haven't really done that work since I left L.A., but I told her I could fill in until the show wraps. It shouldn't be too difficult."

"There's only three dogs left. Just Pepe and Max and Siren Song."

"That is not Siren Song," said Pepe.

"But Pepe thinks there's something wrong with Siren Song. Could she be drugged?"

Felix looked thoughtful. "I could check it out. That's the sort of thing I should be doing. I wonder if that's what Jake was investigating when he was murdered."

Chapter 21

Felix was a star as soon as we walked into the soundstage. He seemed to know everyone and everybody knew him. After all, he had worked as an animal trainer in the film industry for years before moving to Seattle. One of his cousins was a grip, and it turned out that Robyn, the costume designer, was the daughter of his mother's sister's husband's sister.

Then Alice, the vet, came running up. "Felix!" she squealed, and threw her arms around him.

Felix, to give him credit, immediately disengaged from her embrace. He turned to me and drew me closer, saying, "Alice, do you know Geri? I met her in Seattle. That's why I'm down here, to support her. And Pepe, of course!"

"Of course," she said. I saw her look back and forth between me and Felix, and her expression shifted subtly. Had she once gone out with him? "I know Geri and Pepe. In fact, I brought my scanner for her!"

"Hey, I brought mine, too!" said Felix, opening the bag he was carrying and pulling out something that looked like a hair dryer. "It's a 2007 Dataman 40X Scanner."

"Well, I've got a 2009 Minitrack Trojan Scanner," said Alice, brandishing a green item with a big dial in the middle of it. "Mine can read more chips than yours."

"Not true," said Felix. "Let's try them out and see." He called Pepe over to him and ran the hair-dryer-like appliance over Pepe's back. It made a little pinging sound. "Definitely chipped!" said Felix, looking up at me.

"Yum, chips!" said Pepe. "I worked up an appetite dancing. I would like more chips."

Alice pushed Felix aside and swept her green machine down along Pepe's spine. It made a beeping sound as it passed over his neck. "I got a reading, too!" she said.

"What data do you have?" They stood side by side, looking at the gauges on their machines.

"What did you learn?" I asked.

"I do not want Cheetos today. I am craving potato chips," Pepe said.

"Oh, we have to submit the numbers to the registries," Alice said. "It might be twenty-four hours before we get any results."

"I can get mine immediately!" said Felix, and they were off again, arguing about the process.

I left them deep in conversation and took Pepe off to the craft service table to get his potato chips. Of course, he also wanted some of the turkey and cheese, which I put on a paper plate on the floor under the table for him to sample.

"You still owe me some Tofurkey, Geri," he pointed out.

Our next stop was the costume area. Robyn had created a stunning gown for me, a midnight blue satin dress, crusted with sequins around the neckline and hem. It plunged to a deep V in front and an even deeper V in the back. I was pretty happy that Felix had turned up for this particular dance. Pepe was supposed to wear a little black satin tuxedo coat with a bow tie around his neck, and he was not as happy.

From there we proceeded to hair and makeup. I was getting used to being pampered. It was so pleasant to have someone feed me and dress me and style my hair and do my makeup every day. All I had to do was put on a new pair of yoga pants and a camisole in the morning, and for the rest of the day I could just float along and let others take care of me.

As I relaxed with my hair in a basin full of warm soapy water and Zack's strong fingers massaging my scalp, I thought I heard Pepe calling my name.

I sat up abruptly, getting water all over everything. Yes, there it was again!

"Geri! Help!" Then shrill barking and Pepe's voice: "Unhand me, you vicious brute!" That was Pepe, using the language of a telenovella actor, but the terror in his voice was real.

I threw off my towel. The sound seemed to be

coming from the grooming station where Pepe was supposed to be having a bath. It's true Pepe hates baths, but this seemed like an extreme reaction.

I jumped up and dashed around the corner, but Pepe wasn't on the grooming table. I heard his voice again: "Geri, help!" It was coming from the vet's office, which was right next to the grooming station. I ran to the doorway and saw Pepe, standing on a stainless-steel table, shivering, a syringe sticking out of his hide. I surmised that he was afraid to move, afraid the sharp instrument would embed itself farther.

But I couldn't reach him to pluck it out, because my way was blocked by Ted and Felix, who were pushing and shoving each other, and they were surrounded by at least two cameramen with their cameras aimed on the action and the set's still photographer, snapping away.

"What do you think you're doing?" shouted Felix, pushing Ted back with both hands.

"I was trying to help the dog!" Ted protested as he struggled to keep his balance.

"You were trying to drug him!" shouted Felix with another push.

Ted staggered back, bouncing off one of the cameramen and coming back at Felix, his hands raised to ward off another blow.

"She was giving the dog a shot when I came in the room. I tried to stop her!"

"Oh, right!" said Felix. "So who is this mystery person? Where is she now?" He glanced around the tiny room.

"Will you let me get to my dog?" I said, clawing

at the cameramen in my way, but they didn't budge. My hair was dripping down my chest.

"I don't know who she is. I've never seen her before!" Ted said.

Rebecca showed up. To my surprise, she seemed pleased. A crowd of others gathered, alerted by the noise. I saw Alice, the vet, and Robyn, our costume designer.

"You're the one who shouldn't be here," said Felix. "I know all about you. Phony choreographer! Spy!"

"Hey! Just because I'm the one hanging out with your girlfriend while you're up in Seattle picking up dog poop—"

And then the fight was really on. Felix shoved Ted again, and Ted fell against the partition, knocking it over and taking down a light and a mike with it. He got to his feet and launched himself at Felix with both fists swinging. Felix did some sort of complex maneuver where he bent down and Ted went flying over him and landed on the other side of the room, knocking down that partition. He still wasn't done. He got to his feet again and ran straight at Felix, his head down, hitting him in the stomach. Felix went down with a mighty "Oof!" Ted danced around, holding aloft his hands in the victory clasp.

I finally saw my opportunity and dashed around the two men and got to Pepe. I grasped the syringe and jerked it out of his hide, then fell on him, rubbing my face against his fur.

"Are you OK, Pepe?" I asked.

"I think so," he said, but his voice was so small and shivery I could barely understand him.

Felix had gotten to his feet, with a little assistance from one of the cameramen, and now he went after Ted again. Rebecca was directing the cameramen to move around to get a better shot. She was obviously delighted by the conflict.

I began to wonder how much of it was staged. Felix had worked on movie sets all his life. He would know how to fake a fight. Still it sounded real. I heard the thud of a fist on flesh, the moan of pain.

I wasn't sure who was hitting who anymore. I had gathered Pepe up and was holding him against my chest, kissing the top of his head and saying over and over, "Pepe, you're safe now. I'll take care of you." I had been backed into a corner by the fight, and they were getting closer and closer to me.

The syringe had fallen to the floor. Ted stepped on it as he backed away from Felix's flailing fists. The hard plastic caused him to slip. He went down backward, falling against the stainless-steel table and knocking it over. He landed on the syringe itself. "Ouch!" he said. He raised himself up, pulled the needle out of his rump, and then sat back down, an odd expression on his face. A few minutes later his eyes got all glassy and he passed out.

Alice rushed over to him. "Move back, people!" she said. She put her fingers on Ted's neck, checking his pulse. She pulled up his eyelids and examined his eyes.

"Oh my God! What was that?" I asked.

"It must have been pretty strong," said Felix, bending over to pick up the syringe.

"Do not touch," said Pepe weakly. "It is evidence."

"Don't touch it! It's evidence!" I said, passing along Pepe's advice.

"See if you can find the vial that was used to fill this!" snapped Alice, kneeling over Ted. "And someone call nine-one-one."

"Not again!" moaned Rebecca.

Chapter 22

"Let's clear the room!" said Felix, shooing people toward the door. One of the cameramen refused to leave. I saw Rebecca whisper in his ear. This would be great footage for the show.

"Are you OK?" Felix said, coming up and giving me a quick hug.

"I'm fine! But I need someone to check Pepe!" I said. I looked at Alice, but she was busy with Ted, unbuttoning his shirt and pressing her ear against his chest.

"Do you think he needs CPR?" I asked.

"Alice will know what to do," Felix said firmly.

"What about Pepe?" I asked. "If it knocked out Ted, think of what it could do to Pepe!"

"He seems all right," said Felix, looking at Pepe, who was still shivering in my arms. He squeezed Pepe's mouth open and checked his gums. "He's got good color."

"What about you?" I asked. "Are you OK?"

"Felix! I need your help," Alice said. "Find that vial for me."

Felix hugged me again. "I'm fine. I'll send Alice to check on Pepe as soon as she's done here. Once we have the vial, we'll know more."

I found a quiet corner a few yards away, where I could still watch the action. With two partitions knocked down, the room was open to the view. Felix was going over every inch of the floor while Alice tended to Ted, who still wasn't moving.

"Pepe, what happened?" I asked.

"This woman came and took me away from the groomer. She said the vet needed to check me. And then she took me in that room and put me on the table and pulled that syringe out of her pocket and started to stick it in me. That is when I started calling your name!"

"I heard you!" I said, kissing the top of his head. "I got there as soon as I could."

"Well, *sí*, and Ted seemed to hear me, too, because he came rushing in. He had a cameraman with him. And he shouted at that woman. And she went running out of the room. I think Ted was going to pull the syringe out, but he was nervous and he had just put his hands on it when Felix came in and saw him. Naturally he thought Ted was the one giving me a shot, and he pushed him away from me and that is when the fight started."

"So who was this woman?"

"I think it was the woman in the room with Siren Song this morning," Pepe said.

"I wonder who she is," I said. "We've got to find Rebecca and warn her."

"Yes, who knows what she might do?" said Pepe, shivering. "Dog poisoner!"

"How much got in you?"

"I think I am OK," Pepe said, turning around and sniffing his butt where the needle had gone in. "She had just poked it through my skin when Ted came in."

"We need to find out what that was," I said. "Let's go find Rebecca!"

The whole set was in an uproar. No one was where they were supposed to be. The cameramen were filming the revival efforts going on around Ted. People were standing around in groups talking. We saw Max the Poodle and Maxine in their costumes. I wasn't quite sure what dance they would be doing, but Maxine was wearing a skimpy black costume that had little black pom-poms all over it that matched the pom-poms on Max's paws. We finally found Rebecca talking to Miranda in the greenroom.

I didn't beat around the bush. "Who was the woman who was in the room with Luis and Siren Song this morning?" I asked.

"What?" Rebecca looked frightened.

"She's the one who knows what was in that syringe," I said.

Rebecca shook her head. "Impossible!"

"No, it's not impossible!"

"How do you know that?"

"My dog told me."

"Right!"

Miranda's eyes grew wide. "Oh, that explains why you and your dog are so attuned to each other. How fascinating. You will have to tell me how you do that!"

"Seriously, my dog talks to me. And he told me that woman was the one who gave him the shot. Who is she?"

"That's Brandy, Luis's special friend," Rebecca said. When she saw my puzzled look, she said, "Special friend. Like Felix is your special friend."

"He's not my special friend," I said. I hated that euphemism. And I really didn't think it applied to whatever was going on with me and Felix. "So where is Luis? Where's Siren Song? She must be with them."

"I don't know," said Rebecca, "but I'll send someone to find her. You should sit down and relax. You and your dog had quite a fright."

But I couldn't settle down. Pepe and I combed the whole soundstage from one end to the other, but we couldn't find any sign of the mystery woman. But we did find Luis and Siren Song.

They were in the greenroom being filmed about their upcoming performance. "The most important performance of the competition," said Luis to the camera. They were doing a number from *West Side Story*. Luis looked great with his hair slicked back and wearing a leather jacket. Siren Song wore a little pink poodle skirt.

We waited until the interview was done, thinking we would get a chance to question Luis about the groomer's whereabouts, but Rebecca showed up and blocked us.

"Onstage now!" she shouted at Luis and Siren

Song. As they headed out the door, Siren Song turned around and snarled at Pepe.

"Wow! She's really competitive!" I said to Pepe. His tail was between his legs.

"What's going on?" I said to Rebecca. "You've got to ask him about Brandy."

I saw Luis turn around and give us a puzzled look.

"I already asked him," Rebecca said. "She hasn't been around since this morning. She was at the rehearsal hall, but she's never been on the set. Your dog doesn't know what he's talking about," Rebecca said. "Now get in there. We've got to get back on schedule."

"But my dog can't perform until he's been checked by a vet," I said.

"Just do the interview and I'll send someone in as soon as I can," said Rebecca, motioning the cameraman over and whispering in his ear before shutting the door to the greenroom. My hair had never been styled, and my curls were beginning to frizz up all over my head.

"I can't do this," I said to Mark, the guy who usually directed these interviews.

"Rebecca insists we do it now," he said. "We're behind schedule. Even though we allowed some extra time for the fight."

"You mean the fight was staged?" I asked. And here I was all worried about Felix! That rat! He must have been in on it.

"Let's just say we knew something would happen," Mark said. "But it got a little more complicated than Rebecca anticipated. So tell me how you and Pepe are feeling about this evening's performance."

"We feel confident we will win," said Pepe. He sat up straight and turned his snout toward the light. "A little trick I learned from Tyra Banks," he told me. "You must always find your light. That and smizing."

"What the hell is smizing?"

"That is when you smile with your eyes," Pepe said. "Like so!" He looked at me with those big brown eyes fixed on me, his eyebrows slightly raised.

"Can you repeat that, Geri?" Mark asked.

"Oh yes," I said. "We feel confident we will win. . . ." My voice trailed off. Actually, there was no reason to believe we would win. We hadn't even finished our choreography session, and with Ted knocked out, that seemed unlikely. Plus we had not yet rehearsed onstage.

"You don't sound too confident," Mark observed. "Do you want to do that again?"

"There's no way we can win," I said.

"That's not the attitude we want," said Mark.

"But it's the truth!"

"That is not so, Geri," said Pepe, his ears pricked up and his head held high. "We are professionals. We know our steps, and we know how to please an audience. Plus, we are the underdogs. And everyone knows the underdog always wins."

"Your dog seems confident," said Mark.

"My dog is always confident," I said. "If anyone can pull this off, it's Pepe."

"That will do! We just need one good quote. That's a wrap," said Mark.

I was so glad. We tumbled out of the room. I still needed to find the mystery woman, identify the substance she had tried to inject into Pepe, and get my hair and makeup done for the performance.

I returned to the scene of the crime, just in time to see the EMTs moving Ted onto a gurney. He was moving a little. I saw his eyelids fluttering. Alice stood alongside, holding his hand and murmuring, "Just hold on. You'll be OK."

The EMTs gathered up their equipment: used gloves, plastic wrappers, a cotton mask.

"Did you ever find out what was in the syringe?" I asked Alice.

"We found a vial of ketamine. That's a horse tranquilizer."

"Why would someone give that to my dog?"

"Maybe someone wanted to slow your dog down." She saw my confusion. "For the performance."

"Sabotage!" Pepe breathed. "And it came from the camp of *mi amor*. I was going to let Siren Song win, but now I will not. We will take this competition, Geri, and we will win the hundred-thousand-dollar prize and the contract for our own reality TV show."

The EMTs began to roll the gurney toward the outside door. Alice followed along beside it, still holding Ted's hand. I followed after her. We could hear music and cheers and applause coming from the stage area. Apparently one of the contestants was already performing. I wondered if it was Max or Siren Song.

They were taking Ted out through the back door, as exiting through the front door would have disturbed the show. This was the heavy door where I had first met Ted. As we approached, the door burst open and five uniformed policemen entered with guns drawn. They motioned us to the side.

"Move aside," one of them said. "We're looking for Ted Messenger."

At those words, Ted sat up and tried to get off the gurney, but he was strapped in. In the ensuing struggle, the police wrestled Ted to the ground and handcuffed him.

Alice begged them to leave him alone. "He needs to go to the hospital," she said.

Eventually, after consulting with the EMTs, the police agreed that Ted could be conveyed to the hospital, but he was going to be under guard, and as soon as he recovered sufficiently, they were taking him to jail and charging him with murder.

Chapter 23

We finally made it to the costume shop for our final fitting. Everyone was buzzing about the latest developments. Robyn was worried about Pepe, but he insisted he was unharmed by the attempt to drug him.

I slipped into the midnight blue satin dress. The hem and bodice were embroidered with sequins and crystal beads that sparkled whenever I moved. They had a little more trouble with Pepe's tuxedo jacket. They had to make a few adjustments so that he could move easily.

Shelley came bustling in as Robyn fastened a rhinestone necklace around my throat. "You're on in five minutes. And that guy is here to see you again."

It was Jimmy G, wearing a loud and garish red necktie.

"Did you find Nacho?" I asked.

"No, but Jimmy G got a gig as an extra on the

set of *Kiss of Death*," he said with a big grin. "I start tomorrow."

"Congratulations!"

Robyn handed me a pair of long, chandelier-shaped rhinestone earrings to put on. "So have you given up on the package?" I asked.

"Got a new idea," said Jimmy G. "You know how you have to sign in with the guard to get into the movie studio?"

"Yes," I said. Robyn brought over a pair of midnight blue satin high heels, also embellished with sparkles. The heels were higher than any I had worn yet in the competition. "I've been wondering how you get in."

"Just use your name, doll. You seem to be well known here. You and the rat-dog."

I nodded. I was a bit distracted. I pulled at the straps to make sure the shoes were tight. Pepe was meanwhile wriggling as they tried to fasten a blue bow tie around his neck.

"So?" I didn't see the significance. I stood up and tried to balance on those heels. I swayed back and forth and had to reach out to Jimmy G for balance.

"So all we have to do is get the guard to tell us the name of the delivery service, and then we can track them down!"

"Good idea," I said. "I'm surprised you haven't talked to the guard already."

I walked around the room a little. Robyn and her sewing ladies applauded their handiwork.

"Here, help me get to the stage," I said,

leaning on Jimmy G for support. We headed out of the costume room and toward the backstage area.

"Well, Jimmy G tried but ran into a bit of a problem," Jimmy G said.

"Really, what?"

"The guard says Jimmy G is merely a civilian and not entitled to that information."

We reached the partition that separated us from the stage. Shelley materialized with her clipboard. "You're on in ten seconds," she said. "You!" She pointed at Jimmy G. "Get out of here!"

He gave a little tug of his fedora and headed off.

Luis and Siren Song came running by. Luis was shrugging off his leather coat. I could see that he was dripping with sweat.

"Wait!" I said, grabbing Luis by the arm. "I've got to ask you a question."

"What?" He seemed annoyed. Or maybe he just couldn't hear. The audience was still hooting and hollering.

"I've got to ask you about Brandy," I said.

"Who's Brandy?" he asked.

"Your special friend? Who Rebecca flew in from Seattle?"

"Rebecca didn't fly anyone in from Seattle," Luis said.

"Then who was that woman in the room with you and Siren Song this morning?" I asked.

Luis looked around. "I can't talk about that," he whispered. Meanwhile, Siren Song was circling around Pepe, snarling and growling. Luis grabbed her up and went hurrying offstage.

"That was weird," I said to Pepe.

"Yes, that was weird," said Pepe. "Siren Song would not treat me so."

"Perhaps she's in love with Max," I said. The poodle was very handsome.

"No way, Jose!" said Pepe.

Shelley interrupted us. "You're on!"

Chapter 24

The encounters with Jimmy G and Luis had distracted me, but now the realization that we were about to perform hit me.

"Pepe, what are we going to do?" I said. "Ted didn't get a chance to finish the choreography for our dance." And now he certainly wouldn't since he was on his way to the hospital. "And we didn't have time for a run-through." Because of the attempt to drug Pepe and the fight that followed. "And you might be affected by the horse tranquilizer."

"I do feel a little strange," said Pepe. "And there is another *problemo*."

"What is that?"

"Listen!"

And then I heard Rebecca announce, "This is amazing! Siren Song and Luis have scored 9.8, the highest score yet in this competition. That puts them two points above Max and Maxine. Can anyone beat that score?"

"We will have to dance perfectly," Pepe mumbled.

"That's impossible!" I said.

"Not if we dance from our souls," Pepe said. He closed his eyes and swayed a little. Perhaps he *was* feeling the effects of the horse tranquilizer.

The lights went dim, and we scrambled to our places. I was sitting at the bottom of the steps when the music began, and Pepe was sitting a few feet away, looking at me (with longing, I assumed). I was not supposed to look at him until halfway through the dance.

"Just follow your heart," said Pepe as the music began to build.

I got up and began waltzing around the set, my arms held out to an imaginary partner. I could feel the dress swirling and swishing around my legs, could feel it unfurling and curling around me in perfect unison with the music. I was aware of Pepe dancing in tight circles around me, but I was not supposed to look at him; I was supposed to keep my eyes closed.

"Do not fear, Geri," said Pepe. "I will not let you fall."

Ah! If only I could trust him. But he was just a little dog. And I was supposed to be taking care of him. Would there ever be someone who would take care of me?

"A little more to your right," whispered Pepe, passing by me again. The audience was extraordinarily quiet. I didn't hear the usual rustles and murmurs. I wouldn't realize until later how poignant the scene was.

The lighting tech had me isolated in the vast darkness with a blue spotlight, which picked up every sparkle in my dress, while Pepe slipped in and out of the light, a little white orbiting moon. It even gave me a chill when I watched the footage for the first time.

The music dimmed and the singer's voice faltered to a stop. This was my big moment. I curled in on myself, a woman in despair because she believes she is all alone in the world. And, truly, I felt this. My dog might not be my dog. My boyfriend seemed to be interested in another woman. And the man who had been flirting with me had apparently set me up for a fall.

Then the lights began to come up, and the music shifted from minor to major and Pepe came dancing into view, his dark little eyes fixed on me, as they had been throughout the number. We began moving in unison, side by side, his little tux tail swinging behind him, my skirt swirling behind me.

"Step left, step right, and turn two three," Pepe said, coaching me through a series of side-by-side maneuvers. It felt effortless, like we were floating. I was totally able to relax and just copy Pepe's movements.

We danced around each other for a chorus, mirroring each other, and then he hopped into my arms and I caught him and we ended the dance with a series of tight pirouettes.

I stopped, a bit dizzy. OK, really dizzy. The room was spinning around me. I thought I saw the audience leaping to its feet. Then I realized they were. The applause circled around us, growing and growing until it filled the room.

The judges were on their feet, too, applauding. I saw Felix in the audience, his face beaming, and Jimmy G with that big, goofy grin on his face. Robyn and her crew were standing in the wings applauding. Pepe and I took bow after bow and still the applause went on.

The only person who seemed unhappy was Rebecca, acting as MC. She had a sour look on her face as she motioned for us to come stand by her. It took a while but finally the applause died down and Rebecca asked the judges for their scores. I picked Pepe up and held him close.

"What can I say to that performance?" asked Caprice, wiping tears from her cheeks. "That was the most beautiful depiction of the love between a dog and its owner that I have ever seen. They get a ten." Princess yipped in protest, and Caprice tapped her on the nose.

Beverly Holywell looked at Caprice in sympathy and then turned to Rebecca. "I concur. The emotion between the two was so real it simply transported me. This was not an athletic performance. Or an exhibition of good training. This was art. I give them a ten as well."

Rebecca seemed taken aback. She turned to Miranda Skarbos. "Miranda, do you feel the same way?" Her voice was sharp.

"Oh!" said Miranda, clasping her hands and

pressing them against her heart. "If I could give them an eleven, I would! I have never seen such an inspired partnership between a human and a dog. It was as if they could read each other's minds." She leaned forward and said to me, "I think you have the makings of a fine animal psychic. I will take you on as an apprentice, if you like."

"No way, Geri," whispered Pepe. "I do not want you reading my mind."

There was a roar from the audience as they realized what these scores meant. The numbers on the scoreboard flashed and bells rang. Pepe and I had surpassed the score of Luis and Siren Song and had ousted Max from the competition. We were going to the finals! And according to Rebecca, we got a special prize: $5,000 to spend on a shopping spree in Beverly Hills.

Once we were backstage, Rebecca informed us that I should get a really nice dress, as we were invited to a party at Caprice's house. A network executive had seen some of the film from the show and was considering picking it up for his network. Pepe and I would be guests of honor.

I was already in a dreamy state when Felix came running up. His eyes were shining, his smile was bright, his embrace was strong, and his kiss was warm.

"That was fantastic," he told me, still holding me in his arms. "I've never seen a better waltz." He let me go, dropped to one knee, and gave Pepe a pat on the head. "And same goes for you, little amigo." Pepe put both forepaws on

Felix's knee and lapped up the compliment. "There isn't a dog in the world who could have done better."

"I know," said Pepe.

"So," said Felix, rising to his feet. "I have good news for you."

"Beef jerky?" Pepe exclaimed.

"Got the results back from the scan already. No hits! Pepe is all yours."

"Of course he is all mine," I said, picking him up and waltzing him around the room.

Chapter 25

Just being on Rodeo Drive intimidated me. The storefronts were dazzling with white stucco walls and arched windows. The street was immaculate, with neatly spaced palm trees and trimmed bushes sporting white flowers. The names of the stores represented the highest echelon of design and price: Dolce & Gabbana, Versace, Christian Dior, Louis Vuitton, Prada, Ralph Lauren, Tiffany & Co., and Chanel.

Pepe seemed to know his way around. He went running down the street and dashed into the open door of a boutique just as a customer left: a rather disheveled young woman in sweatpants and sunglasses, with her hair wrapped in a turban. I almost ran into the door as I turned around to stare at her. Surely she was someone famous. Only a movie star would dress like that on Rodeo Drive.

By the time I got into the store, Pepe was all the way in the back, by the dressing rooms, sitting on a gray velvet tufted sofa. He looked like he was holding court. He was surrounded by a bevy of salesclerks: skinny young women in chic black dresses.

"Pepe! You're back," said one.

"Where have you been?" asked another.

"We missed you so much," said the third.

Pepe was chattering away, but I'm not sure they understood him because they kept talking to him.

They looked up as I approached. Then they looked behind me, out to the street. Seeing no one with me, they turned back to Pepe.

"Where's Caprice?" they asked.

"I am no longer with Caprice," said Pepe, though his voice sounded sad. He looked at me. "I am now a star on reality TV, and this is my partner, Geri."

One of the salesgirls approached me, her hand held out. "Are you Caprice's assistant?"

"No, I'm Geri Sullivan," I said. "And this is *my* dog. His name is Pepe."

"I'm Chloe," she said. "And we know Pepe. He's our favorite customer. So did you say you work for Caprice?" She looked over my outfit, and I could see the puzzled look on her face. "Are you her stylist?"

"No, I don't work for Caprice," I said. "Pepe is my dog." It was nice to be able to say that with confidence. "We're here to buy a dress."

"For Caprice?" asked another one of the salesgirls.

"No! This has nothing to do with Caprice!" I knew my voice was getting shrill. "The dress is for me."

"This is not the best place to buy a dress," Pepe said. "But we will begin here." He leaped off the couch and went running over to the rack.

"This is how he does it," said Chloe, trailing behind him. "Which one, Pepe?"

Pepe sauntered down the line of clothing and kept glancing from the dresses to me. "Not the right color," he said. "Not the right shape."

Every so often he would put out his little paw and tap a dress. Chloe would instantly remove it from the rack and hand it to one of the sales-girls, who ferried it to the dressing room.

"That should do for a start," said Pepe when five dresses had been chosen. He settled back on the sofa where the salesgirls plied him with petit fours, and I was whisked away to the dressing room where one of the stylists (they called them-selves stylists), named Zan, was designated to assist me. I hated the idea of removing my clothes in front of this twenty-year-old with her perky breasts and bone-thin torso, but I had no choice. She wrestled my dress rehearsal clothes off of me, dropping them into a pile on the floor, and helped me step into the first gown. It was tomato red, with one asymmetrical shoulder strap and a lot of draping in the long skirt, which split to reveal my legs. It was movie-star glam-orous and all wrong on me.

"Come, let's show Pepe," said Zan.

"I don't know." I turned back and forth, in-specting myself in the mirror, but eventually I was persuaded to go out. A little crowd of cus-tomers had gathered, which made me even more self-conscious.

"Oh! That will look smashing on Caprice," said Chloe as soon as I emerged from behind the screen. Apparently they still thought I was a stand-in sent by Caprice to try on dresses for her. Rather flattering. I wouldn't mind having Caprice's figure. But what would look good on her waiflike body would look ridiculous on me. Pepe agreed.

"All wrong!" he said. "That is not the one."

"How much is this dress?" I asked as Zan helped me wriggle out of it.

"Seven thousand, five hundred," she said.

"Oh my God!" I stumbled in surprise and stepped on the hem of the skirt, just as Zan was picking it up to put it back on the hanger. I thought I heard the fabric rip. Zan saw my horrified face. "Don't worry. It will just go on Caprice's expense account."

I tried to tell her again I was not with Caprice, but she would not listen to me.

"Let's go with something less expensive," I suggested.

Zan next helped me wriggle into a black dress that looked like a series of bandages wrapped around my torso. It did make me look a lot slimmer but sort of like a sausage that had been poured into a tube, with my boobs spilling out at the top and my legs seeming enormously long as they emerged from the micro skirt. Pepe dismissed that dress as well.

In this fashion, we went through all five dresses, and then Pepe indicated it was time to go. He jumped off the sofa, bowed to the salesgirls, and trotted in front of me out onto the sidewalk.

"That was horrible, Pepe," I said. "I hate shopping for clothes."

"I know," said Pepe. "That is why you buy all your clothes at those awful places that smell of poverty and old hand cream."

"Value Village is not a horrible place," I insisted. "It is very fashion forward in Seattle to wear vintage clothes."

"Perhaps in Seattle. But in Los Angeles, you must dress like the Los Angelenos." He glanced back at me. I was wearing the yoga pants and tank top I had worn to the rehearsal. He gave a little sniff, as if the clothing smelled bad, then pawed at the door of another boutique.

The same scene was repeated here, with the salesgirls—or I should say, stylists—greeting him with enthusiasm and assuming I was sent by Caprice to pick up some gowns. Again I tried on several dresses, none of which suited me, and we made our departure.

"Now we are ready for the real thing!" declared Pepe, turning down a side street. "I know just the place to find your dress."

"Why didn't we go there first?" I asked as we stood outside a small shop with an arched window. Window boxes outside the shop were planted with trimmed hedges. The awning was green and white striped. A bell rang as we stepped over the threshold. It was much smaller and darker than the first two stores.

"We were just warming up," said Pepe. "Those

were places that I used to shop with Caprice. But I think you will be happier here."

At this store it was different. The owner, a buxom blonde who wore a strange yellow and black striped silk blouse over tight knit pants, fawned over Pepe, but she did not call him by name. And Pepe went around pointing with his paw at dresses, which were much more to my taste. They were handmade and one-of-a-kind, using recycled fabric, according to the store owner. And I got to try them on by myself instead of being assisted.

The first dress was flattering. The second dress really accentuated my curves. And I fell in love with the third dress. It was made out of a transparent silver fabric with an overlay of black lace. It had a fitted bodice and a loosely gathered skirt. Beads glittered in the bodice, and the hem was finished with a heavier band of fabric that gave the skirt a weight that made it swing in the most delicious way. I twirled in front of Pepe.

"I think that is it!" said Pepe. "You look radiant."

"I feel like a movie star in it," I said.

"As well you should, Geri," said Pepe. "We are only one performance away from fame and fortune."

The dress was well within my price range. I had enough left over to buy a pair of strappy silver sandals that totally complemented the dress. I sailed out of the shop with my packages and Pepe, feeling on top of the world.

Pepe and I had the highest scores on *Dancing with Dogs*. My sexy boyfriend was taking me to a party in Beverly Hills. And Pepe was really my Pepe, despite what some Beverly Hills shopgirls thought.

Then Pepe said something that made my blood run cold: "Too bad Caprice was not with us. Those shopgirls could have told her I was her dog."

Chapter 26

Back at the hotel, I took a shower, then slipped into the silver and black lace dress. I felt a little strange in it, like I was an imposter, pretending to be someone rich or famous. I put on the silver sandals and twirled around in front of the mirror. Pepe did his best to give a little wolf whistle, but it came out as "Woohoo!" Pepe can't whistle, and I've never heard him howl either.

Felix was waiting for us down in the lobby when we descended the stairs. He looked magnificent, in a gunmetal-gray jacket over a black T-shirt and black jeans. He gave a wolf whistle. He didn't have any trouble whistling. I'm not sure about howling. Maybe someday I'll find out.

He ushered us into the car he had rented: a silver Toyota Prius. Leave it to Felix to eschew Hollywood glitz for something economical and environmentally friendly. I had a fleeting moment of nostalgia for Ted's sleek black Jaguar, but I had to admit Felix's values were closer to mine. And, of course, he made Pepe sit in the back.

The party was in full swing when we arrived. This time we were inside the house, in a huge living room, decorated with velour armchairs, velvet sofas, gilded tables, and gold silk drapes framing the windows. A huge chandelier sparkled over a gilt dining room table that was covered with trays of appetizers. In the next room, guests lined up for drinks from two handsome bartenders who worked behind a bar that looked like it came straight from a Paris club.

Rebecca introduced me to Don Hillman, the CEO of the network interested in picking up the show.

"One of our finalists," Rebecca said. "It was a complete surprise. The poodle was favored to win. But that's what's so delightful about these shows. We got some early audience feedback that they loved the Chihuahua, so we were able to make sure he progressed in the competition."

I wanted to protest that Pepe and I had won fair and square, despite the obstacles thrown in our path, but I kept my mouth shut. Not Pepe.

"The best dog will always win," he announced.

"This little guy does have quite a lot of character," said Mr. Hillman, patting him on the head. "One can almost imagine him announcing that he intends to win the whole thing." He gave me a kiss on the cheek and patted Pepe on the head again before allowing Rebecca to whisk him away to meet some of the other key players.

As soon as I put Pepe down, he went running over to Caprice and tried to get her attention. This time Caprice, who was sitting on a sofa deep in conversation with Miranda Skarbos and Beverly Holywell, called Jennifer over and handed her Princess so she could put Pepe on her lap instead.

"He reminds me of my Chihuahua," Caprice said, kissing him on the top of his head. "In fact, he had the same name, Pepe. But my Pepe ran away about a year ago. He was my favorite dog. I still miss him every day."

"I did not leave you on purpose," said Pepe, licking her cheek. "Something happened, although I do not remember exactly what. All I remember is darkness and then being in dog jail."

"Oh!" Miranda cried out. "Can I do a reading for you and let you know what happened to him?"

"That would be wonderful," said Caprice. "You can't imagine how much it hurts, not knowing."

"Do you have anything that belonged to Pepe?" Miranda asked. "It should be something he was particularly fond of. An item of that sort gives off the strongest residual vibrations— allows me to make the best connection when trying to channel the dearly departed."

"Humph," said Pepe. "I do not mind the 'dearly' reference, but 'departed' I am not!"

"I don't know," said Caprice. "I was so crushed when he was gone that I got rid of everything that was his. I just couldn't bear being reminded of him. He was so special to me."

"I am still special," said Pepe. "Everybody says so."

"Wait," Caprice continued. "There is Pepe's old Squeaky."

"My Squeaky!"

"He dearly loved his Squeaky—it's a little stuffed bear that squeaks when you squeeze it. I keep it on a shelf in my bedroom by his photo. Just a minute—I'll get it for you."

Caprice left the room, and Pepe ran over to the small settee that Felix and I were sharing by the fireplace.

"My Squeaky!" he cried once more. "Oh, Geri, I am so excited to see my Squeaky again."

"He's pretty excited, isn't he?" said Felix.

I leaned down toward my dog, who was virtually turning cartwheels at my feet.

"Pepe, you never told me you liked squeaky toys. I could've gotten you one."

"*Gracias,* but there has been only *uno* Squeaky for me, Geri," he said. "Now and forever."

"Oh."

Caprice came back in holding a small, rather scruffy-looking brown bear. "Here it is," she said, handing it to Miranda.

Pepe dashed over just as Miranda took it from Caprice. "Mine! Mine! Mine!" he yelled, leaping up and clamping his teeth onto one end of it. He then began a tug-of-war with Miranda, a struggle punctuated with squeaks.

"Oh my," Miranda said as Pepe pulled it toward him and she pulled back on it. *Squeak! Squeak! Squeak!* went the bear.

"Pepe!" I scolded.

"No, that's OK," Miranda told me as she continued her tug-of-war with Pepe. "I feel very strong vibrations from this toy. They are incredibly strong—some of the most intense I have ever felt!"

"They should be," said Pepe, but he lost his grip on the bear when he spoke. He looked up at it sadly. Miranda was placing it against the middle of her forehead.

"*¡Ay, caramba!*" Miranda exclaimed when it touched her. She pulled it away as if it were red-hot and held it before her eyes. "How odd! I wonder why I said that?"

I could have told her that Pepe was able to speak Spanish. But wouldn't that mean that my Pepe was really Caprice's Pepe? I didn't want to believe that.

"Yes," said Miranda. She held the toy bear up almost prayerfully. "I need quiet, please. Total silence."

Everyone in the room became quiet. All except Pepe, that is, who kept jumping up and down in front of Miranda. "Give me back my Squeaky!" he said over and over again. "I want my Squeaky!"

I went over and grabbed him.

"But I want—"

"Shhh," I told him. "She's trying to channel you."

"That is *loco*," he said. "I am right here."

"Ooooooooh," Miranda moaned, her eyes closed, her tone somewhere between pain and pleasure. "The small white dog is near . . ."

"Is that not what I just said?" Pepe told me.

Caprice sat down, her eyes on Miranda, and Princess jumped up into her lap.

"Yessssss," said Miranda, almost swooning in her chair. Then she sat up bolt straight and quivered slightly as she spoke. "I feel his presence. He is with us."

"Of course I am. I'm right here in the room!" Pepe said.

"He is speaking to me. He is giving me a message to give to you, Caprice."

"What a fraud," said Pepe. "Nobody but you can hear me speak, Geri."

Miranda swayed back and forth. "Your Pepe is beyond the Rainbow Bridge, Caprice," she said.

"What Rainbow Bridge?" asked Pepe. "Where is this bridge? I don't remember crossing a bridge."

"Oh!" gasped Caprice. She clutched Princess close.

"Yes, I am sorry to say he has crossed over," said Miranda.

"What does that mean?" asked Pepe. "What did I cross?"

"But he wants you to know that he loved you very much."

"Of course I love her!" said Pepe. "Why is she talking about me in the past tense?"

"Hush!" I said. "She is not talking about you. She is talking about a dog that died."

That shut him up. He sat down and studied Caprice with a curious look on his face.

"Oh, my Pepe," said Caprice. Tears began to fall from her eyes. "How did it happen?"

Miranda closed her eyes and was quiet again, lifting her head and moving it from side to side as if trying to listen to whispers.

"He says it was an accident. An auto accident."

There was a gasp, and I saw Jennifer put her hand to her mouth.

"It happened right in front of the house. He ran out into the street. He was hit by a car."

"Oh, my poor darling!" cried Caprice. She glanced over her shoulder at Jennifer. "You knew about this?"

Jennifer's eyes went wide. "We didn't want to upset you."

"It was painless," Miranda said quickly. "He wants you to know he didn't suffer. His last thought was of you."

Caprice cried out. I had not really expected such deep feeling from her. But she seemed to be in pain.

"She is telling lies, Geri," said Pepe. "Tell her it is not true. I am right here."

"I can't, Pepe," I said.

"Well, if you won't, I will!" He trotted over to Caprice and pawed at her legs. She patted him on the head while she watched Miranda, stricken.

"I am alive! I am right here!" said Pepe.

I don't know who was more pathetic. Pepe, so frantic to get her attention, or Caprice, with tears running down her cheeks, leaving behind the tracks of her mascara.

"He says his life with you was very happy. You made him very happy."

"Can you give him a message from me?" Caprice asked.

Miranda nodded.

"Tell him I loved him more than any dog I have ever owned," Caprice said. Pepe, at her feet, whimpered. Princess, in her lap, whined.

"Oh, and he has another message for you," said Miranda, her head cocked to one side. "Do you believe in reincarnation?"

"I don't know," said Caprice. "Maybe."

"Well, Pepe says that he loved you so much that he arranged to come back to you in the form of Princess."

"Could it be?" said Caprice, holding up Princess and shaking her to and fro. "Are you my Pepe?"

"Ridiculous!" snapped Pepe. "Of course she is not. I am right here."

"He will always be with you. He will never leave you," Miranda said.

"I will call you my Princess Pepe from now on," said Caprice, showering the Papillon with kisses.

"*¡Ay caramba!*" said Pepe. "How could she confuse that prissy dog with me? I would never come back as a Papillon."

"Don't you get it, Pepe?" I asked. I was about to explain to him that this proved he was not really Caprice's dog. But then I realized how this would make him feel. Did I have to spoil his illusions? He liked to believe he had once lived with a movie star.

Chapter 27

Felix took me back to the hotel so I could leave Pepe in the room while we went out to dinner. I figured he was feeling sad, and I really didn't want to leave him. But I didn't want to miss my chance for a romantic date with Felix either.

"I'll leave the computer on for you," I said, setting up my laptop.

I took the opportunity to freshen up and redo my makeup. Pepe sat on the bed watching me as I reapplied my lipstick.

"Where are you going to dinner, Geri?" he asked. "Spago? Nate 'n Al's?"

"I don't know," I said. "Felix made the reservations. But you're not going with us."

Pepe hung his little head. He tipped his head to one side and stared at me out of those big brown eyes. "But I am your partner." He is so good at looking sad. Perhaps he learned that from the telenovellas he watched.

"True," I said. "But it is illegal for a dog to be inside an establishment where food is served."

"An unenlightened society!" he declared. "In France—"

"I know," I said. I had heard his stories before about going to France, but now I didn't believe them. He was my dog. He had never been to France with Caprice. And maybe someday he would accept that reality.

"Look," I said, kissing him on the top of his velvety head. "I'll bring you back something in a doggy bag. How's that?"

"Humph!" Pepe could be quite expressive in his disdain. He turned his head to the side and laid it on the bedspread. "Doggy bags are for mere *perros*."

Felix had chosen a restaurant that was situated in a house in one of the canyons with a terrace that looked out over the Pacific Ocean, a vast darkness now that the sun had set. The patio was lighted with orange and red and pink lanterns. Candles flickered in orange glass holders on the tables. The scent of sagebrush and the briny smell of the ocean mingled in the air. The effect was magical.

Felix greeted the owner, a glamorous-looking blonde, with a hug and two kisses. I recognized her as an actress I had seen in several of my favorite TV dramas. According to Felix, he had worked with her on a movie. She introduced us to the chef, a shy Frenchman who was also her husband, and sent a complimentary bottle of champagne to our table.

"Have you seen your family yet?" I asked Felix after we were seated. I knew he had grown up in L.A. and had moved to Seattle only within the past year.

"No, it's been such a whirlwind since I got here," said Felix. "But I was planning to stay over an extra day after the filming is over and see them. I'd love for you to meet them."

Wow! Was this moving too fast? But then I had taken him to dinner at my sister's house on our first official date. "Sure," I said. "I'll have to check with Rebecca. She flew us down here, and I'm not sure what arrangements she made to get us back to Seattle."

"How is she doing?" Felix asked as the waiter brought us a plate of appetizers: celery rémoulade for me and some seared scallops for Felix. He knew that Rebecca's husband had only recently passed away.

"She seems to deal with grief by staying busy," I said. "She's at the rehearsal hall before we get there. She spends all afternoon at the sound-stage, overseeing every little detail. She's the MC during the filming. And at night she does meetings, trying to come up with a new twist that will help keep the show interesting."

"Like bringing me down," said Felix.

"Yes, I guess that's a common trope in reality TV shows," I said. "I hope it wasn't too awkward." I still didn't know if he had heard me call him Ted.

"What was she doing hiring an animal activist to be a choreographer?" he asked after polishing off one of his scallops, followed by a big sigh. He offered me the other one on the tip of his fork, but I waved it away. I don't eat shellfish. I did offer him a bite of my celery rémoulade, which was silky and flavorful. It was delicious with the champagne.

"I don't think she knew he was an animal activist at first," I said, casting back in my mind for clues. "But in the end she must have known." I thought of that conference I had interrupted in her living room.

Felix shook his head. "So he was pretending to be a choreographer?"

I felt called upon to defend Ted. "He had been a dance instructor at one time. We got some of our highest scores on the dances he choreographed."

"Yes, but the whole invisible partner thing was Rebecca's idea," Felix said.

"It was?" I was shocked.

"Yes, she told me about it when she was prepping me to go into the room," Felix said.

That was disappointing. And here I thought it was Ted who was so observant about my longing for a partner. Had he been instructed by Rebecca to flirt with me just for the cameras? It was a distinct possibility.

The waiter appeared with the bottle of wine, a Pinot Noir that Felix had chosen to go with both our meals. He had ordered the short ribs served on polenta with a tomato confit and pea shoots, while I was having cod, lightly baked and served with figs, artichokes, and fennel.

For a while we were both too busy tasting all the various elements on our plates and trying them out with sips of the wine. Then he asked me about the last few days. And I started talking. I told him about the package for Jimmy G and how Jimmy G had come down from Seattle to try to find it. I told him about how Pepe and I had discovered the show was rigged. I described Pepe's concern about Siren Song.

"Did you ever get the results of that test on Siren Song?" I asked as the waiter cleared our plates.

"Oh, that's right," Felix said. "Alice left me a voice mail earlier. I should probably call her back." He got up and excused himself. He came back at the same time as the dessert, but nothing could sweeten the sour look on his face.

"What's wrong?'

"Alice has been at the hospital with Ted. He recovered enough so they could cart him off to jail. Alice is pretty upset. She says anyone who loves animals as much as he does could not kill a human being."

"That makes some kind of sense," I said. "But his love for animals seemed so excessive that maybe he could harm a human if he thought that person was going to harm an animal."

"Is that true for any of the people who died?"

"I don't think Nigel had anything to do with animals, except for his dog being missing. And

Jake was there to protect the animals on the set. But Ted hated him because he said he didn't do enough."

"There's been tension between PETA and the Humane Society. PETA doesn't think the Humane Society does enough, while the Humane Society thinks the PETA folks are too radical."

"Still, it's hard to see how that would turn into murder."

We were both silent for several minutes. Felix stared down at his gelato. I toyed with my panna cotta. I thought I knew what was wrong. Maybe Felix still had feelings for Alice. Maybe that was why he had rushed down to Los Angeles when Rebecca invited him to the show. And now it was obvious to him she was developing feelings for Ted.

"So what's bothering you?" I finally asked.

"Geri, I have some bad news," he said.

My stomach turned. Which was not so good considering all the delicious food I had just eaten.

"What is it? Is it about Siren Song?"

"That's part of it. Alice got back the results of the drug test she did. Siren Song tested positive for steroids."

"That would explain why she was acting so aggressively and why she smelled so different to Pepe." I took a bite of my panna cotta. Felix did not pick up his own fork.

"There's more, isn't there?" I asked.

"I don't know how to tell you this." His eyes were dark. With pity? With compassion?

"What?"

"It's Pepe."

"What about him?"

"Alice got results from the registry she checked. Pepe is registered."

"How can that be? You said he wasn't registered."

"I'm sorry, Geri. There are four different registries. I checked three of them. Alice checked the other one." Felix reached across the table and took my hands in his. "Pepe belongs to Caprice Kennedy."

I stared at Felix and shook my head. "No, it can't be."

"I'm sorry, Geri. I know how hard this must be for you. You love him so."

"Then how could he have ended up in a shelter? Wouldn't they have checked him for a chip?" I was desperately seeking a way out of the nightmare.

"Sometimes they miss these things. Or maybe they checked the wrong registry. Like I did."

I stared at him, my mind working frantically. Was there any way out? Maybe I didn't have to tell Caprice. Maybe I didn't have to tell Pepe. Only Felix would know. Actually I'd have to break up with Felix because I couldn't bear to be around him. I couldn't live with the knowledge that I had misappropriated a dog. But I couldn't bear the thought of living without Pepe either.

Chapter 28

Needless to say, our date did not end well. When the evening started, I had hoped it would end with Felix in my bed. Instead it ended with me kissing him good night in the parking lot. I watched Felix drive away with tears running down my cheeks, then tiptoed up the back stairs to my room.

Pepe was asleep, curled up on one of the pillows, with the TV on. I thought he might wake up when I entered, but he didn't even stir. Which was maybe for the best. He would know right away that I was upset and would want to know why.

All along I had been afraid that Pepe really was Caprice's dog. Now I knew the truth. How could I give him up? How would he react when I told him? But I realized I was being selfish. Caprice obviously loved him as much as I did. And she had so much more to offer. How could my small condo in rainy old Seattle ever compare to her mansion and staff of caretakers in balmy Beverly Hills?

And that was just it, I thought. It was the life he'd been accustomed to before spending his few short weeks with me. If I really loved him, I'd have to do the right thing no matter how much it hurt. But I could wait to tell him, maybe until after the competition was over. I didn't want to get him too distracted on our last day. And the truth was, I wanted to enjoy one more day with him.

I went to turn the computer off, and when I hit the mouse, a video started playing. Pepe had figured out how to use the webcam and had posted a video of him in the hotel room. He was barking away. It almost seemed like he was talking. His inflections and expressions made you think you could understand what he was saying.

For the first time, I saw what other people probably saw when they saw my talented dog. Was it possible that's what he was doing all along? And was I just interpreting his very animated yips and yaps to what I wanted to hear? Which was that I finally had a partner, someone to care for me and protect me, someone who would love me with no reservations.

It was bittersweet: going through our morning routine, knowing it was for the last time. The special twist for this last day was that Rebecca had decided both teams were going to do the same dance: a tango. So we had only half as much time as usual with our choreographer. But that was fine. After running through our routine for a while, we had enough time to help Jimmy G with his scheme to get his hands on the MetroLand Studio logs.

His plan was crude and simple, rather like Jimmy G himself.

He positioned me and Pepe near the Metro-Land main gate and told us to wait until a car approached. Then my job was to distract the guard by approaching and asking him a question. Meanwhile, Pepe ran out in front of the on-coming car and pretended that it hit him, rolling off to the driver's side, yipping and howling in faux pain.

"Oww! My leg is broken like a chicken bone!" he screamed at the top of his lungs. "And my head is cracked like an egg! It feels like castanets are going off inside it!"

The driver naturally got out of the car to see what he could do. I dashed over and started crying about my poor dog. And, as we hoped, the guard left his post and ran to Pepe's side to try and help.

Jimmy G darted into the empty guard shack and swiped the logbook while the guard was distracted. He was in and out in a flash.

"Oh, I am feeling better now," said Pepe when he saw that Jimmy G had made his score and was safely out of sight.

I picked Pepe up and told the driver and guard, "I think he's better now." I patted Pepe's head. "Aren't you, little amigo?"

"I deserve an Oscar!" Pepe said.

"Are you sure?" the guard asked me.

"Positive," I said, strolling away with my dog.

"And a Golden Globe, too," said Pepe.

A few minutes later, we were outside our soundstage, sitting on a bench with Jimmy G while looking over the logbook's pages.

"Good plan your boss came up with, huh?" said Jimmy G.

"Without my thespian talents, it would have been a fiasco," said Pepe.

"Did it ever occur to you that the guard will quickly notice that the logbook is gone?" I asked my boss.

"No, Jimmy G didn't think of that," he said.

"Well, I think you better get it back before they start searching the lot for it," I suggested.

We pored through the pages. The guard book was just a standard composition notebook with ruled lines. To the left was the date and time, and on the next line the name and affiliation of the person. For instance, I was happy to read my name: "Geri Sullivan, Soundstage 13, *Dancing with Dogs* participant." I wondered how Ted was listed and I paged back to the previous day. He was listed as "Ed Galliano, Soundstage 13, *Dancing with Dogs* choreographer." So he must have created a fake ID.

"Did you find the name of the package delivery service?" Jimmy G asked.

I had completely forgotten what I was looking for. I paged back a few more pages. "Here's an entry," I said. "For Hollywood Parcel Service on Wednesday at five p.m."

"Jimmy G was already here on Wednesday," he said. "Are you sure that's right?"

"It says, 'Soundstage Thirteen, package for Luis Montoya.'"

"Maybe they deliver a lot of packages to the studios. Check for Monday. That's the day you called Jimmy G."

I paged back to Monday. "Yes, here it is again. Around three p.m. Hollywood Parcel Service, Soundstage 13, delivery for Geri Sullivan."

"Well, there you go!" said Jimmy G. "Hollywood Parcel Service. Jimmy G's going to go check them out."

"And give the logbook back to the guard," I told my boss. "Just tell him you found it lying on the ground. Pepe and I have to go get ready for our final performance." In more ways than one.

Chapter 29

As soon as we walked into the soundstage, Pepe was on high alert.

"Something is wrong, very wrong," he said.

"Another murder?" I asked.

"No, not a murder. But almost as bad. Someone has made Caprice very sad."

He went running off in the direction of the special lounge where the judges congregated when they weren't actually in the judges' box. Rebecca was standing over Caprice, who was curled up on the sofa, with her face in her hands.

When she looked up as we entered, I could see her skin was blotched red and her eyes were puffy. She had been crying hard, for a long time. "I just can't go on!" she said. "I'm just too stressed out."

"You have to go on," Rebecca said, waving the paper. "Your contract says you must complete all five days of work to get your payment."

"I don't care about the payment. How can you

even talk about money at a time like this?"
Caprice's voice was screechy.

"Plus we can assess punitive fees to cover the
cost of replacing you and reshooting all of the
judging scenes," said Rebecca.

"How can you expect me to work when my
precious dog has been kidnapped?"

"Kidnapped? Does she think you kidnapped
me, Geri?"

"Hush! I think she's talking about Princess."
The Papillon, usually in Caprice's handbag or
on her lap, was conspicuously absent.

"Yes! My Princess! My precious Princess Pepe!"
Caprice wailed. She didn't even seem to notice
my poor Pepe, who went running over to com-
fort her. He leaped into her lap and tried to lick
her chin. She stroked him idly with one hand
while dabbing at her eyes with the other.

"My dog was kidnapped and I didn't break
down!" said Rebecca.

"Your dog was kidnapped?" Caprice looked
up, startled.

"Siren Song was kidnapped?" Pepe asked, his
ears twitching.

"When?" I asked.

"A few days ago," Rebecca said. "And did I
start crying like a baby? No! I got a dog to replace her and went right on with the show."

"I told you, Geri," said Pepe. "That dog was
not Siren Song. That dog is an imposter."

"How did you replace her?" I asked.

"I found a similar dog in Orange County, who
already knew how to dance. I had to dye her fur
a little to make her look more like Siren Song."

So Pepe was right. Why was he always right? So annoying.

"So it was Siren Song that Miranda could sense at the murder scene!"

"Yes, I guess so," said Rebecca.

"Well, then maybe the murder was related to the kidnapping," I suggested.

"I told you so," said Pepe.

"It's possible," said Rebecca. "At any rate, when I got the ransom demand, I informed the police. They are looking into it. I trust they will get my dog back. Meanwhile I did what I had to do to keep the show going."

"Geri! This is serious!" said Pepe. He jumped off Caprice's lap and ran over to me. "We must rescue Siren Song." He looked back at Caprice. "And Princess, of course."

"And that's what you should do," Rebecca continued, turning back to Caprice. "Inform the police and let them handle it. Pull yourself together for the judging. You only have to be on camera for an hour." She gave Caprice the once-over. "You should get yourself into makeup. You look awful." And she marched out of the room.

"I can't call the police!" wailed Caprice. "The kidnappers said if I called the police, they would kill my poor Princess Pepe."

I saw Pepe wince every time Caprice used that name. Still he was determined to help her.

"Offer our services, Geri!" he said.

"When did this happen?" I asked.

"This morning," said Caprice. "Jennifer was walking her around the block and a van drove up. A guy jumped out, shoved Princess into the car, and took off."

"This sounds familiar," said Pepe. "Something like this happened to me once."

"This is not the time for one of your stories," I told him.

"What stories?" asked Caprice.

"Never mind," I said. "Did Jennifer get a good look at him? Or the car?"

"No. She said the guy wore a black ski mask. And the van was white."

"How do you know it was a kidnapping?"

"I got a call asking for ransom. About an hour later. After I had fired Jennifer."

"You fired Jennifer?"

"Yes, I mean, she let my precious Pepe get run over by a car. And then she let some guy steal Princess right from under her nose."

"Good! I never liked her," said Pepe. "She is part of that bad memory."

"What do they want?" I asked.

"They want money! That's no problem. I've got it right here." Caprice patted the bulging red patent leather purse sitting next to her on the sofa. "The problem is the delivery. I'm waiting for a call now. They said I had to come alone. And Rebecca says I can't leave. And my manager says I can't go without a bodyguard."

"Those shopgirls thought you were a stand-in for Caprice. You could pretend to be her," Pepe said.

"What if we delivered the money for you?" I asked.

"How could you do that?" Caprice asked.

"I could pretend to be you. We have all the tools we need right here in the costume shop and in makeup."

"Say you will drive her car, Geri!" Pepe said.

"I could drive your Ferrari, too," I offered.

"That is brilliant!" said Caprice. She leaped up and hugged me. "If you get Princess Pepe back, I'll give you a reward. I can't believe you would do this for me."

That was generous of her. And I had to admit that I was secretly hoping that if I gave her back Princess Pepe, it would make it OK for me to keep *my* Pepe.

"Oh!" she said suddenly. "But you can't do it. You have to perform."

"That's true," I said, sobered. "It's the final performance. All the other dogs have been eliminated."

"Except for the imposter," Pepe said.

"Pepe would hate it if we missed the final performance."

"Especially if that fake won instead!" Pepe said. "But we have no choice, Geri. We must help Caprice. Fame and fortune are nothing when we can save the life of a precious dog."

Caprice was overjoyed. She gave me the dress right off her back (it was a sparkly short silver number that reminded me of tinfoil) and borrowed another dress from Robyn in the costume area. Robyn outfitted me with a pair of sparkly heels, a blond wig, and a pair of sunglasses to complete the disguise. In fact, it was so effective that when Jimmy G came strolling into the costume shop, he thought I was Caprice. The real Caprice was in the makeup area trying to conceal the effects of her grief.

"Where's Geri?" he asked Pepe.

I had to take off my sunglasses and my wig before he could recognize me.

"It's great you're here," I told Jimmy G. "We need your help."

"Well, Jimmy G needs your help as well," he said. "Turns out that Hollywood Parcel Service is just a front. Tried to go to the address they gave and found it's actually about a mile out in the Pacific Ocean. Something fishy is going on."

Just then, Caprice came running up, waving her cell phone. "I just got the call. They want me to meet them at three p.m. at the La Brea Tar Pits at the Giant Sloth statue. I described what I was wearing—I mean what *you're* wearing. And I told them if they didn't give me Princess first, I wouldn't give them the money."

Chapter 30

We pulled into the main parking lot at the La Brea Tar Pits at about a quarter to three. I was driving Caprice's red Ferrari and Jimmy G was going to meet us there. He was driving his rental car. It was crowded on a Friday afternoon, and I had to keep driving around looking for a parking spot. I was pretty nervous. Even though we had given ourselves plenty of time, I was worried about being late for our appointment with the dognapper.

I wasn't sure whether to be happy or frustrated that he had chosen this spot for our meeting. At least it was public, so I didn't think we would be in any danger. And I had always wanted to see the Tar Pits, not to mention the museum next door. Not much chance of that, with so much at stake.

As if reading my mind, Pepe said, "You would love the Tar Pits, Geri. They contain bones going back eons, including the bones of my largest forebear, the dire wolf."

"Since when have you been interested in paleontology?" I asked.

"Since Caprice took me here for the first time and I saw the skeleton of that fearsome beast at the museum."

"Oh," I said. "I'm glad you had such a good time the last time you were here." I was annoyed by how often he brought Caprice into the conversation. "But this is serious—"

"*Uno momento*, Geri," he said. "I am most serious. Deadly serious. Some of my formidable ancestor's blood still courses through my veins. When I get my paws on that dognapper, I will attack as ferociously as any dire wolf!" For emphasis, he reared up at the side window and loosed a terrifying "Grrrrrrrrr!"

When we finally found a parking place, Pepe was still in wolf mode. He bounded out of the car, growling, but stopped abruptly when he got to the edge of the parking lot.

"Holy guacamole!" he said.

"What is it, Pepe? What's the matter?"

"The *ninos*," he said. "They are everywhere!"

He was right. The green lawns that surrounded the low-slung museum were covered with laughing, running, crying children. Dozens of them. Pepe is not afraid of much, but he is afraid of children. He began to shiver.

"Don't worry, Pepe," I said, picking him up and gently stroking his back. "You'll be safe with me."

Four kids picked that moment to run up to us, yelling, "Can we pet your dog?"

"No, he'll bite!" I said, a little more sharply than I intended. Their parents, who had caught up with them, frowned at me, then shooed their offspring toward the parking lot.

When the juvenile storm had passed, Pepe looked up at me and said, "Geri, tell me you are not planning to have *ninos* of your own someday soon."

"No," I told him, even though at age thirty-two, I felt my biological clock starting to tick down.

"*Bien*," he said. "*Muy bien.*"

We began wandering through the park. We were waiting for Jimmy G to arrive, although we had already agreed that he wouldn't approach us, since he might scare off the kidnapper. Also we needed to find the Giant Sloth. The park was dotted with large metal sculptures depicting the various creatures that had once roamed this part of L.A.: lions, saber-toothed tigers, and a huge woolly mammoth just to name a few.

I was surprised to see puddles of black tar in the grass that we had to avoid. I'd thought the Tar Pits were surrounded by a big fence or something.

"Do not be concerned, Geri," said Pepe. "This stuff only bubbles up from the ground here and there. The puddles are not deep, just nasty if you get your paws in them."

"Is that right? Well, what about that one?" I asked, pointing at some tar that was about four feet in diameter with a small fence around it.

"*Sí*," said Pepe. "That one could indeed be

deep. Like they say, there is always an exception to the rule."

Jimmy G was supposed to make himself inconspicuous, but he was hard to miss in his green sports coat and a brown fedora with an emerald feather. But although he was quite noticeable—people actually turned and stared as he strolled around the park—he pretended not to know us when we caught sight of him.

Finally we spotted the Sloths. Two of them, made out of some kind of brown metal. The one in front stood up on its hind legs, looking around.

"It is bueno that they were supposed to be slow. I would not ever want a thing like that to grab me," Pepe said.

The Sloth was much taller than me. I stood in the space between its arms, looking out across the park to see if I could spot the dognapper. But what did a dognapper look like?

"What is our plan?" asked Pepe. When I shrugged he said, "How about this: When you are talking to him, I will circle around and bite him in the Achilles tendon. That will bring him down. With any luck, we will get the *perrita* back and keep the ransom!"

"I don't like that plan!" I said. "We aren't going to confront this creep. We just want Princess back! As long as he delivers her, we're going to let him walk away. So don't do anything foolish!"

"What about Siren Song?" asked Pepe.

"You're right! But I doubt that he'll bring

feet out into the grass and starting to sniff and circle. "I do not pick the time—it picks me."

"Great. Just great." I scanned the park. I didn't think I would recognize the dognapper, but I could keep my eye out for Princess. The park was full of dogs: a black Lab chasing after an orange Frisbee, a little terrier being carried by a dapper gentleman, two dachshunds getting tangled in their leashes.

A man was approaching with a small furry dog on a leash. The dog was the same size as Princess, but her fluffy coat was a dirty brown.

"Pepe!" I cried. "Hurry up! I need your help!"

"This is most inconvenient," said Pepe. He centered on one patch of grass and gave it a really good sniff. "Ah, this is the spot," he said, then squatted down.

The man was short and round, with a peculiar bounce in his step. He had a round face and a fringe of wispy beard.

An older woman walking by scowled at me. "I hope you're going to clean that up, young lady."

the Sloth. I thought he was going to pull a gun on the guy, but instead he raced toward him.

"I'm going to report you to the authorities," said the woman, pulling out her cell phone. She glared at Pepe as she headed off, punching in numbers. If she called the cops, that would scare away the dognapper.

"Nacho!" said Jimmy G, falling on the guy and giving him a big clap on the back. "I've been looking for you everywhere, man. Fancy running into you here!"

Siren Song along. So we'll have to follow them back to their lair."

"Put me down!" said Pepe. "I want to be ready for this dognapper. We are on time, are we not?"

"Yes," I told him, glancing at my watch. "We're a couple minutes early, in fact."

"*Bueno,*" he said, "because I must relieve myself."

"Now? Of all the times to use the bathroom, you pick *this* moment?"

"I am a dog, Geri," he said, moving about six feet out into the grass and starting to sniff and circle. "I do not pick the time—it picks me."

"Great. Just great." I scanned the park. I didn't think I would recognize the dognapper, but I could keep my eye out for Princess. The park was full of dogs: a black Lab chasing after an orange Frisbee, a little terrier being carried by a dapper gentleman, two dachshunds getting tangled in their leashes.

A man was approaching with a small furry dog on a leash. The dog was the same size as Princess, but her fluffy coat was a dirty brown.

"Pepe!" I cried. "Hurry up! I need your help!"

"This is most inconvenient," said Pepe. He centered on one patch of grass and gave it a really good sniff. "Ah, this is the spot," he said, then squatted down.

The man was short and round, with a peculiar bounce in his step. He had a round face and a fringe of wispy beard.

An older woman walking by scowled at me. "I hope you're going to clean that up, young lady."

She pointed at the pile Pepe was making and started to repeat herself. "I said, I hope you're going to—"

"Go away!" I yelled at her. I was never rude to people, but the short guy with the dog had stopped in his tracks, maybe thirty feet away, and looked very suspicious. "Just go away!" I yelled even louder.

"Well, I never," said the woman, taking a step back.

Just then Jimmy G jumped out from behind the Sloth. I thought he was going to pull a gun on the guy, but instead he raced toward him.

"I'm going to report you to the authorities," said the woman, pulling out her cell phone. She glared at Pepe as she headed off, punching in numbers. If she called the cops, that would scare away the dognapper.

"Nacho!" said Jimmy G, falling on the guy and giving him a big clap on the back. "I've been looking for you everywhere, man. Fancy running into you here!"

Chapter 31

"What?" Nacho looked confused. He looked at me and then at Jimmy G.

"The package, man," said Jimmy G. "Jimmy G's been trying to find the package!"

"You weren't supposed to come down to L.A. to get it, you idiot!"

"What? And not collect the money you owe Jimmy G?"

"Are you still going on about that? I told you a million times, I don't owe you nothing."

"What were you saying, Geri?" Pepe asked, kicking up a bunch of grass to cover his leavings.

"Look who's here, Geri!" Jimmy G said, wrapping his arm around the guy's shoulder and pushing him toward me. "My old buddy from my platoon, Nacho. We called him that because he ate Nacho Cheese Doritos all day long!"

"Is that Princess?" I asked Pepe. The dog at the end of the leash didn't look like the proud creature I had last seen in Caprice's arms. This dog had matted fur and was a splotchy brown color.

Pepe bounded over to her. The dog let out a high-pitched whine and struggled against the leash, rushing forward to meet Pepe. They had a quick consultation, nose to nose, then nose to tail. Nacho spun around, trying to keep Pepe away from her.

"Hey, lady, watch your dog," he said. "Don't you know he's supposed to be on a leash?"

"*Sí*, it is Princess, but she has been mistreated," Pepe said, trotting back to me. "See how they have tried to alter her appearance!"

"So, Nacho is the dognapper," I said. I didn't mean to say it so loud, but both Jimmy G and Nacho heard me.

"Dognapper?" said Jimmy G.

"You know her?" said Nacho, looking back and forth between me and Jimmy G.

"Yeah! She's in disguise, but she's my Gal Friday."

"Associate!" I said.

Nacho took a few steps back and managed to break Jimmy G's hold. He picked up Princess and held her tight against his chest. "Take one more step and I'll break her neck."

We all froze—that is, all except Princess and Pepe. Princess twisted her head around and nipped Nacho's hand just as Pepe charged around and sank his teeth into Nacho's ankle.

"Ow! Ow!" He dropped Princess, who was still attached to the leash, and kicked at Pepe, who deftly avoided the blow.

I had to do something, so I smacked him on the head with Caprice's purse.

"Ow!" He doubled over.

I saw Jimmy G reach for the gun he kept in a shoulder holster, but Nacho grabbed Princess, holding her by the neck.

"Back off or I'll snap her little neck!" Then he took off running. Princess twisted and turned in his grip, but he held her in such a way, she couldn't bite him again.

"Princess!" Pepe and I screamed at the same time.

Jimmy G sprinted after him, yelling, "Give it up, Nacho! You never could outrun Jimmy G!"

"Come, we must save her!" shouted Pepe. He took off running and I followed as quickly as I could.

We must have been quite a sight—Nacho huffing and puffing with Princess held out in front of him, Jimmy G in his bright green sports jacket and fedora waving his pistol, a small white Chihuahua at his heels, and me bringing up the rear, wearing a sparkly silver dress, high heels, and sunglasses.

"Call the police!" I screamed to no one in particular. All I got in return were stunned expressions from various onlookers. Possibly everyone thought we were a guerrilla art troupe. I saw people snapping photos. Good! There would be evidence if we didn't manage to snag Princess.

Nacho reached the fenced-in area surrounding the biggest of the tar pits and began circling around it. We all followed. Out of the corner of my eye, I caught glimpses of the tableaux inside the chain-link fence. A huge woolly mammoth trumpeting as it was dragged down into the pit. Another mammoth sinking to its knees with the fangs of a saber-toothed tiger embedded in its neck.

After completing a circuit of the tar pit, Nacho headed off, with Princess still clutched to his chest, toward a circular structure. He disappeared inside it, followed by Jimmy G, then Pepe, and eventually me. As they ran in, onlookers ran out. I saw the words OBSERVATION PIT over the door as I rushed in after them.

The structure was open inside, with overhead lights and wooden scaffolding that surrounded a pit some twenty feet in diameter. Nacho and Princess were on the far side of it, with Jimmy G advancing on them from the left and Pepe coming at them from the right.

"Nowhere to run, Nacho! Give it up!" yelled my boss.

Pepe growled—a *real* growl, no doubt channeling a dire wolf—and stalked toward Nacho, his fangs bared.

Princess, seeing her opportunity, struggled wildly. Nacho was distracted and lost his grip on her. She managed to wriggle out of his grasp, but in the process she went tumbling over the edge of the barrier. There was a splat as she landed in the tar pit below.

"Princess!" I shouted, and looked around for a way to reach her.

"What the hell's going on up there?" I heard a voice coming from the pit.

I looked over the wooden railing and saw

two men, about fifteen feet below, who were kneeling on boards that ringed the pit. They were evidently digging fossils out of the hardened edges around the tar pool at the bottom.

"Oww! Damn!" I glanced up again and saw Pepe biting into Nacho's ankle as Jimmy G put him in a headlock.

Pepe jumped back just as Nacho twisted away and tumbled into the pit.

"Hey!" said one of the archeologists, jumping back as he was splattered with tar. "You could have just damaged fossils that are millennia old."

Nacho didn't seem to care. He was trying to extricate himself from the tar. He was in up to his knees, and every time he tried to lift his leg, we could hear a horrible sucking sound.

One of the archaeologists had managed to scoop out the struggling dog. I scrambled halfway down the ladder that led into the pit, and he handed her up to me. She was half covered with tar and whimpering, I think, with embarrassment.

"It's OK," I told her as I carried her up the ladder. "We'll get you back to Caprice." Pepe came running over. He must have told her the same thing, I think, because she stopped whimpering.

"Call the police!" said one of the archaeologists.

"Get the dog back to the car," my boss ordered. "Jimmy G will help get the bastard out and meet you there."

"We are not leaving without Siren Song!" said Pepe.

"I don't think she's here," I said. "He only brought one dog." I leaned over the edge of the pit. "Do you have Siren Song?" I asked.

"Up yours!" he said.

"I will find her," said Pepe. "Take me back to where we first met with him and I will track backward."

Chapter 32

I carried the tar-splattered Princess as we headed back to the Giant Sloth where we had first met Nacho. Pepe began sniffing the ground, zigzagging back and forth as he traced Nacho's path to the parking lot.

"This is it!" said Pepe, pausing in front of a white van that had backed into the parking space so the rear doors faced the park. I looked at the side and saw the words HOLLYWOOD PARCEL SERVICE painted in blue.

"Oh my God!" I said. "It's the van they used to make deliveries to the studio."

"This is the van they used to kidnap Siren Song!" said Pepe. "I can smell her from here." He jumped, trying to reach the back doors. "Geri, help me. Open the door!"

It was one of those vans with two rear doors, each one with a window. I set Princess down, grabbed a handle, and pulled it open. As the door swung open, Pepe jumped inside. At the same time, I saw the silhouette of someone's head in the driver's seat. What had I been thinking? Of course Nacho would bring backup, just like I had.

"Pepe! Watch out!" I said. "There's someone in the van!"

But it was too late. The driver had seen me and turned the key in the ignition. Meanwhile, Pepe was sniffing along the metal floor of the van. There was no sign of Siren Song, although there was a big plastic dog carrier in the back. Perhaps she was inside that.

The van jolted forward, and I saw Pepe slip on the metal floor. His claws couldn't get any traction. Then the van zoomed out of the parking lot with Pepe in it.

No way was I going to lose my dog. I picked up Princess and ran for the red Ferrari. I pulled out of the parking lot in time to see the white van taking a left and heading down the street. I wasn't sure if the driver had seen me. But just in case, I pulled off the wig and the sunglasses, thinking that might fool them. Princess cowered in the passenger seat. She was a sorry sight, all dirty and spotted with tar.

The Ferrari was fast and I was able to keep the van in sight. One of the van's rear doors was swinging open and I could see Pepe sliding back and forth in the cargo area as it wove through traffic at high speed. I'd never driven so fast on a surface street—thank God for the Ferrari.

I managed to keep up with the van for the first few miles, almost clipping a car or two in the process. One time the van braked, then sped up abruptly, causing Pepe to slide precariously close to the edge of its open back door. His forelegs were thrust stiffly out in front of him as he barely stopped himself from tumbling out onto the street. I don't know if he saw me or not, as I was about four car lengths back, but his normally bulging eyes bulged out even farther and his mouth opened wide like he was saying, "Help!"

The van took a hard right turn—took it so fast that I thought it would roll over. This caused the rear door to swing shut and stay shut. At least Pepe wouldn't be able to fall out now, I thought, following at such speed that my car fishtailed a bit as I came out of it and hit the gas again. (Where were the cops when you needed them?)

Then, much to my relief, the van slowed to a normal speed and obeyed all the traffic laws and lights for the next five or six miles. My guess was that the driver bolted away from the Tar Pits in a panic when I tried to enter the van but finally slowed down when he thought it was safe—which meant he must not be aware that I was following him.

At one red light, I stopped only a couple feet behind the van. I wanted to jump out of the car, run up to the van, yank the door open, and rescue Pepe. But no sooner had I tried to

unbuckle my seat belt than the light changed
and we took off again.

Damn. Damn! When would they stop for good?
And where would that be?

My question was answered a few minutes later.
We had entered a part of town that was mostly
residential. The streets were lined with older
apartment buildings. Many of the ground-floor
windows had bars.

The van rolled to a stop in front of an apartment building that might have once been hot
pink but was now a faded coral. It was L-shaped
and three stories tall, with walkways that ran in
front of every apartment door along each
floor. The building had faded turquoise trim
and doors. The name LAGO VISTA APARTMENTS
stood out in cursive letters against a backdrop
of river rock.

I parked about two cars back. I wasn't quite
sure what I was going to do, but I knew I had to
get to Pepe. I could hear him yelling from inside
the van. Although his words were muffled, the
message was clear. He was furious.

Then I heard the car door slam. The driver
jumped out of the van and went toward the
apartment building. As soon as I saw him, I knew
who it was. Hard to miss that porcupine hair or
the vivid purple Hawaiian shirt. *Rodney Klamp!*
The getaway driver was Rodney Klamp.

Without even looking back, he scrambled
up the open stairs on the left side of the building. I watched him emerge on the second-floor

walkway and enter an apartment about three doors down.

When I was sure he wasn't coming right back out, I jumped out of the car and ran to the van.

"Pepe!" I cried, and pulled open the rear door.

"Pepe!" I said with relief when I saw that he seemed unhurt.

"Pepe!" I cried for a third time when he bolted out of the van and, nose to the ground, made a beeline to the apartment building's stairs. "What are you doing?"

"I am hot on the scent of that lily-livered dog-napper, that betrayer of *perros,* that scoundrel!" he said. He raced up to the second-floor landing, and I ran after him screaming, "Pepe!" yet again.

"I am coming for you, Rodney Klamp," Pepe growled. "And when I find you, I will clamp my jaws around your leg like a juicy drumstick."

I caught up with my dog just as he threw himself against the apartment door Rodney had entered.

I pulled my tiny avenger away from the door, but it was too late. The door jerked open and Rodney stuck his head out. "What the hell's going on out here?" he said.

"This!" yelled Pepe, barreling in at him.

I was right behind Pepe as he went through the door. I thought I heard another dog barking when I got inside the apartment, but was too distracted by my own dog attacking Rodney to give it much thought. Pepe aimed for Rodney's ankle and sank his teeth into his flesh. Rodney began hopping around and screaming. "Get it off of me!"

What to do? I wished I had some way to threaten Rodney, but I didn't own a gun. The police. I needed the police. I lunged for the phone I saw on the bar that divided the tiny kitchen from the living room.

I couldn't help noticing the décor. Left over from the fifties, like the apartment building. Nubbly beige drapes. Fake maple colonial-style dining table. A boxy brown sofa. Two suitcases by the front door.

"What the hell?" A young woman emerged from the back room. It was Jennifer, Caprice's personal assistant. She was dressed in jeans and a striped top, and she was carrying a small pet carrier. I realized that the barking I'd heard ever since we burst in was coming from that travel cage. It had to be Siren Song.

"Get it off me!" Rodney kept screaming, dancing around and trying to smack Pepe who was attached to his leg like a remora to a shark.

"What do you expect me to do?" asked Jennifer. "I don't even like dogs."

I was scared for Pepe, but he seemed to be holding his own for the moment. So I decided to rescue Siren Song while I had the chance. I tried to grab the pet cage away from Jennifer. She held on.

"You can't have her," she told me. "This Pomeranian is our movie money."

"No, you idiot!" yelled Rodney, now trying to kick Pepe off of him like he was some kind of soccer ball. "Get it through your head—Siren Song's worthless. That bitch doesn't care about getting her damned dog back. Let her have the dog and help me!"

"Huh?" mumbled Jennifer. She hesitated for a moment, and I won our tug-of-war. But I hadn't expected her to let go so easily, and the pet carrier dropped to the floor. The cage door flew open on impact and out popped Siren Song. She seemed unharmed. She was a little bedraggled but otherwise in good shape. She headed toward Rodney, growling.

"I'm getting out of here," said Jennifer. "I never should've gotten involved with you two idiots."

"No, you're not going anywhere." I got hold of her shoulders and tried to push her against the wall. She pushed back and we went down, rolling around under the dining room table. She was strong and wiry, and she had a lot more to lose than I did. She slapped me in the face, and I punched her in the nose, and she pulled my hair and I pulled her hair, and then she butted me in the jaw with her head. I flopped backward, hitting my head against the wall.

Jennifer scrambled to her feet. I tried to move, but my head swam and stars swirled through my field of vision. Jennifer jumped on top of me.

At about the same time, Rodney managed to kick Pepe free. My little white dog came flying through the air, hit the wall beside me, and, with a horrible crunching noise, fell to the ground, where he lay still and silent.

Chapter 33

Siren Song ran over to Pepe and sniffed at him. He didn't move.

"You killed my dog!" I screamed.

"Screw him!" Rodney shot back. "He was killing me!"

"My God," said Jennifer, staring at the blood gushing from Rodney's ankle. "You might need stitches."

"I'll take care of it later," Rodney told her. He went into the other room and came back with the belt from a terry-cloth bathrobe. "Tie her hands behind her back." He rolled me over and Jennifer tied my wrists together. They hauled me up and propped me in a sitting position. I could see Pepe, a few feet away. He was totally limp. Siren Song sat beside him and whimpered.

"Where's her purse?" Rodney asked. "Check to see if she's still got the ransom."

"No, I don't," I lied. "I gave it to Nacho."

"Where is Nacho?"

"Stuck in the tar pits," I said with some satisfaction.

"She didn't have a purse with her when she came in," said Jennifer. "She must have left it in the car."

"Well, go check!"

"How would I know which car is hers?"

"Figure it out! You've got to be good for something besides whining!"

While Jennifer was gone, Rodney hobbled around, looking for something to staunch the blood pouring from his ankle. "Ow!" he yelled, limping badly.

I looked over at the still form of Pepe. I couldn't tell if he was breathing or not. "Stay with me, little guy," I whispered.

Rodney went into the bedroom and began throwing things around. He came out with a suitcase just as Jennifer hurried through the front door waving the red patent leather purse.

"She stole Caprice's car," she told Rodney. "And Caprice's purse."

"She loaned them to me," I said.

"Doesn't matter," said Rodney, taking the purse away from Jennifer. "We're in luck. Looks like the ransom is all here. A cool quarter of a million dollars!" Rodney pulled out one of the neatly bound stacks of $100 bills. "Ha!" He pushed it back into the bag. "One thing you've got to say about Caprice. She cares about her dogs."

"More than her employees," said Jennifer bitterly.

"We've got what we need. Time to get on the road," Rodney said.

"What if she called the police?" Jennifer asked.

"Yes," I lied again, my head still spinning. "I called the cops!"

Rodney glared at me. "I don't think so. She wouldn't have come in here alone if she had," he said.

No, he was right, I wouldn't have come in alone, except to protect my dog.

"Anyway," he told Jennifer, "if we leave right now, we should be able to make it across the border in a few hours. With all that money, we won't have any worries. We can finish our movie and submit it to Sundance."

"That's what this is all about? You killed my dog for a movie?"

"Not just any movie," said Rodney. "This is art. We're going to be rich and famous."

Jennifer pointed at me. "Not if she tells the cops about us."

"She won't get a chance," said Rodney.

"What do you mean?" Jennifer asked him.

"What do you think?"

A look of horror spread across her face. "You don't mean—"

"Look, I'd rather not do it. But she's a loose end."

"I can't believe it," said Jennifer. "That's your solution for everything. Kill Nigel when he won't pay the ransom. Kill the guy who's trying to protect the Pomeranian. You guys have bungled everything right from the start when we tried to kidnap Caprice's Chihuahua last year."

"That was Nacho's fault!" Rodney said. "He's too impulsive. We're better off without him."

"Well, I'm not going to have any part in murder," said Jennifer.

"Look, if you don't like it, go start the van." He reached into his pocket and tossed her the keys. "Take the suitcases." I noticed he didn't let go of the purse containing the ransom. "I'll be down in a minute."

"What about the dogs?"

"We don't need them anymore."

"You're not going to hurt them, are you?" Nice to know she had empathy for the dogs, if not for me.

"No, I'm not going to hurt them. Just go!"

Jennifer looked at the keys in her hand, then at me. "Well, OK," she said. She grabbed the suitcases and headed out the front door.

Siren Song put her forepaws on my thigh and whined softly as if there was something I could do for poor Pepe, who lay so still beside me.

Rodney went into the kitchen and I could hear him opening drawers and cursing. When he emerged, he had a sharp steak knife in his hand.

He held it up in one hand like some crazed killer in a horror movie and approached me.

Siren Song bared her fangs and growled ferociously at Rodney. Pomeranians always look happy, even when they're growling, so she didn't seem like much of a threat.

Rodney kicked her. She yipped and went tumbling across the floor, a furry golden ball.

"Now for you," said Rodney. He didn't sound too confident. In fact, he swallowed hard as he looked down at me.

"I know you're not a killer," I said. "Just let me go and I promise I won't say anything."

Rodney's eyes were sad. "It's too late for that," he said.

He bent over me, the knife raised above his head. Suddenly there was a horrific snarl—it sounded like a dire wolf must have sounded—and a golden ball of Pomeranian came flying through the air and chomped onto Rodney's upraised arm. "Ow! Ow!" he yelled, waving his hand back and forth. Siren Song stayed attached. He dropped the knife.

I saw my opportunity, lifted up my legs, and aimed both feet at Rodney's crotch. I was still wearing the high heels, so the impact was brutal. Rodney let out a squeal like a slaughtered pig and fell to his knees in front of me. I rolled over on top of the knife, managed to grab it with one hand, and started sawing away at the belt around my wrists.

Rodney was still gibbering, but I didn't

know how long he would be incapacitated. If he recovered before I got free, I would be a goner. Like my dog.

Just then Pepe rose from the dead. Maybe he had been playing possum.

I was overjoyed to see him stagger to his feet. And even more happy when he charged Rodney and clamped his jaws around Rodney's wrist, chewing viciously. It sounded like Pepe was trying to say something while he bit down, but it just came out as *Grrrr! Grrrr! Grrrr!* Rodney screeched even more when Siren Song let go of his arm and bit him on the butt. And then a strange ugly gray dog came running out of the back room and joined the fray. It must be Nigel's dog, Kooky! She started scissoring Rodney's already-bloody ankle with her sharp incisors. He howled in pain, rolling back and forth on the beige-colored shag carpet that was becoming spotted with his blood. I was so glad it wasn't mine.

At that moment, Princess the Papillon appeared in the doorway, her white fur spotted with tar. She must have jumped out of the Ferrari and made her way to the apartment. She assessed the situation and realized she could be most effective helping me. She rushed over and began yanking on the bathrobe belt. Within a few minutes, I was free.

I staggered to my feet. The dogs were doing a job on Rodney—Princess had joined in— but they needed help. He now had a Chihuahua attached to his wrist, a Pomeranian on his butt, the Chinese crested on his ankle, and a Papillon chewing on his ear. I took hold of one of the captain's chairs around the dining room table and waited for my opportunity. When Rodney rolled over onto his hands and knees and tried to push himself up, I bashed him across the back with it. Unlike the chairs that break apart on impact in the movies, this one didn't. It made a terrific *thunk!* and sent Rodney crashing forward like a felled tree. I was ready to do it again, but he lay there unmoving, his face planted firmly in the shag carpet.

Pepe ran to Siren Song. "*Mi amor,*" he said, nuzzling her repeatedly. "I have saved you!"

"And *muchas gracias, amiga!*" Pepe said, turning to Kooky, who pranced with happiness. She was even uglier in person than she was in pictures, but I could see why Nigel was so attached to her. She had a lot of personality.

"Your timing was impeccable," Pepe said with a courtly bow for Princess.

So much for my part in it, I thought.

"And my partner—" Pepe began, turning to me.

Then the front door flew open and in stepped Jimmy G.

"Have no fear! Jimmy G is here!" he announced. After giving the scene a brief scan, he added, "Oh! Looks like you've got it pretty much under control."

"How did you find us?" I asked.

"Nacho squealed like a little pig," said Jimmy G. "The police are on their way. I just beat them to it. Had to come to the rescue of my operatives."

"What about Jennifer?" I asked. "She's—"

"Handcuffed to the steering wheel in the van," said my boss. "Don't worry. Stick with Jimmy G, kid! You'll go far."

Chapter 34

Jimmy G stayed behind to guard Rodney and talk to the police. I gathered up all the dogs. We raced to the soundstage in the red Ferrari and got there in the nick of time. They were already filming the opening of the show. The theme song was playing. Rebecca, in a tight, short, gold lamé dress, was introducing the judges and announcing the prizes.

I set Princess on the floor backstage, and she went running down the stairs, across the stage, and straight for Caprice, who was sitting in the judge's box. I heard Caprice's cry of joy as Princess leaped into her arms, whimpering and covering her face with kisses. Caprice held her close, even though the tar still matted on the dog's fur was rubbing off on her white dress.

Siren Song did not head for Rebecca. She stayed with me and Pepe as we went into the costume area. Kooky came along, too. Perhaps the two dogs had become attached while they were in captivity.

I shrugged off the silver dress, and Robyn helped me into my red tango dress. It was wicked—with a deep slit up the front and an asymmetrical hemline that fluttered when I moved. Pepe was buttoned into a little double-breasted jacket.

We could hear the music of the tango. Luis must be onstage with the fake Siren Song. Felix caught up with us as we hurried over to the backstage area, with Siren Song following. Kooky had stayed behind in the costume area. Robyn was enchanted with the ugly little dog and was fawning over her.

"Where have you been?" Felix asked. "I've been looking for you everywhere."

"We had important business to take care of," I said. "I'll tell you all about it later."

We could see the dancers onstage. Luis was wearing a double-breasted coat, similar to Pepe's, while the fake Siren Song wore a red dress that fluttered around her fluffy tail.

"Hey," Pepe told the real Siren Song, who stood next to him. "There is the dog who has taken your place! We cannot let her—"

Pepe didn't get a chance to finish his sentence because Siren Song let out a furious growl and dashed onstage, barking and biting. The next thing we knew, the fake Siren Song went running past us, all of her red ruffles trembling, with Siren Song in close pursuit.

Luis stopped and stood in the middle of the stage, stunned.

Then Siren Song came running back and circled around Luis, her tail twitching seductively. She backed him up, step by step, until he was on the edge of the stage. Then, with a quick flick of her tail, she turned her back on him.

Pepe went running forward to meet her in the center of the stage.

Luis seemed even more confused.

"What's happening?" said Rebecca, taking a couple steps forward.

"You want me to cut?" the main cameraman asked.

Any inclination Rebecca may have had to stop the cameras was cut short when the dogs began dancing with each other, and the audience roared its approval.

"No," Rebecca yelled at the cameraman. "Keep rolling! This is really good stuff." She waved her hand at Luis. "Get out of the way!" He stepped off the stage.

Both Pepe and Siren Song stood on their hind feet, faced each other, dipped slightly as if bowing, and then began to circle each other. They mirrored each other's movements, turning in a wide circle but always keeping their eyes on each other. The music swelled and became more complex, with numerous little runs and syncopations. Their little feet flew and flashed as they stepped into each other. Siren Song flung her head back. Pepe swaggered around her. And then as the violins played a final melodic flourish, they rested their heads on each other's shoulders and stood, poised in embrace, as the music died away.

The audience came to its feet, all the judges included, clapping, hooting, whistling, cheering. In the wings, Felix hugged me and I kissed him.

Pepe and Siren Song dropped to all fours and walked to the lip of the stage to take their bows.

Rebecca bounded up the steps, beaming. She turned to the judges. "Judges," she said. "We've obviously had an impromptu change to the program. What do you—"

"I give them both a perfect ten!" said Caprice, clutching Princess in her arms. "That was the most magnificent and heartfelt dance I've ever seen!"

"Ten to both dogs!" echoed Miranda. "They expressed the true essence of the tango: desire, passion, two hearts beating as one."

"I have to concur," said Beverly. "It seemed totally spontaneous. And they did it all without the benefit of any signals or supervision. They both deserve a ten!"

The audience went wild.

"Well," said Rebecca, "we've heard the decision of our judges. It's time to add up the total points for both of our finalists and award the grand prize. Remember the winner gets a hundred thousand dollars, an all-expense-paid trip to the Westminster Dog Show, and an opportunity to star in their own reality TV show."

"Hold on," said Caprice. Then she motioned to her fellow judges to sit down and confer with her. After a brief consultation, Caprice stood and said, "We judges are all agreed. There should be no *single* grand-prize winner. The grand prize for

Dancing with Dogs should go to *both* Siren Song the Pomeranian and Pepe the Chihuahua!"

The audience erupted with applause so loud and with such terrific cheers that it almost drowned out Rebecca's formal announcement. Pepe and Siren Song took bow after bow.

I was so happy for them, especially for my dear Pepe. I stood with Felix, his arm around my waist. I glanced across the audience and saw that Caprice was smiling just as warmly as I was. She obviously loved Pepe very much, and it made me feel a tad better regarding the news I still had to break about Pepe being her long-lost dog.

I wiped away a tear, knowing I would remember this moment forever.

Chapter 35

After the audience left, we all gathered backstage. The catering crew brought in trays of appetizers and handed each of us a flute of champagne. Everyone was there: Robyn and her costume ladies, who had dressed Kooky up in a little turquoise tutu and tiara; Reynaldo the groomer (although he disappeared with Princess to try to remove the tar from her fur); Zack, my hairstylist; and Alice, the vet, standing by Ted; I guess he had been released from jail. All the other choreographers were there as well, along with the other contestants and their dogs and the three judges.

When all our glasses were filled with bubbly, Rebecca proposed a toast.

"I want to thank everyone who made this show possible," she said. "Thanks to your talent and hard work, my dream of making *Dancing with Dogs* a hit show is now a reality.

You persevered despite all of the difficulties. I salute you, one and all!"

We raised our glasses high, then took a sip. It was good champagne.

"*Nada* for me?" asked Pepe, who stood beside me with his ladylove, Siren Song.

"Dogs can't drink champagne," I told him. "It wouldn't agree with you."

"So you say." He was offended. "I have had tequila once and it was fine. Although I did not like the lime."

"One more thing," said Rebecca. "A special toast to all of our fine contestants and their partners. Learning new dances every day couldn't have been easy, but you performed with great style and poise. Especially our grand-prize winners, Pepe and Siren Song. Your final dance was more than I could have imagined in my wildest dreams!"

We all took another swig of champagne.

"Now you *must* give me a taste of your champagne," Pepe told me. "After all, she is toasting me!"

"Oh, all right." I knelt down and let him slurp some from my mostly empty glass.

"Yuck!" he said, sneezing and shaking his head. "The bubbles go right to my nose."

"And last but not least," Rebecca went on. "Don Hillman just informed me that the network wants to sign us to a three-season contract. And they want to begin the first season with this pilot. So, soon all of you who participated will be famous! Plus, of course, you'll earn residuals every time the show is aired."

This brought quite a roar of approval from the contestants present who had been eliminated during the competition. (The cheering came from the dogs' dance partners, of course, as they themselves acted, well, like dogs, most of them eager for any canapé or tidbit of cheese that might fall to the floor.)

"OK, everybody," Rebecca said. "That wraps it up. Enjoy yourselves, but don't forget—we still have to break everything down, clean up, and vacate the soundstage by midnight at the latest."

We gave Rebecca a big round of applause when she finished. She took a bow, then made a beeline directly for me.

"I guess I have you to thank for finding Siren Song," she said. "How did you do it?"

"We were looking for Caprice's dog. The same people had kidnapped Siren Song."

"Well, I'm so glad she's safe," said Rebecca, picking her up and holding her close. "Ugh!" She held her out at arm's length. "She smells awful."

"She does not!" said Pepe. "She smells delightful. As good as liverwurst!"

"Look what they did to her," said Rebecca. "She's filthy! What sort of people were they?"

"The sort of people who had no trouble killing people for money," I said.

"Oh, my poor darling!" said Rebecca, showering Siren Song with kisses. "At least they didn't harm the dogs."

"Yes!" One could be grateful for that.

"I have to say I was really angry with you when I heard that you had taken off just before the final performance."

"We figured it was more important to rescue the dogs even if we missed performing in *Dancing with Dogs*."

"Well, I don't agree with your priorities," said Rebecca, "but it all worked out in the end." She buried her face in Siren Song's fur, then crinkled her nose.

"Siren Song, you're going straight to the groomer for a shampoo!" She turned to me. "Don't forget. We're flying out tomorrow at two p.m. You and Pepe are going with us, right?"

"About that . . . ," I said, but then I looked around for Felix and saw he was on the other side of the room talking to Alice. Maybe I wouldn't be staying an extra day to go meet his parents. And certainly Pepe wouldn't be with me.

"Let's meet for lunch just after checkout time. Then we'll take the limo to the airport," Rebecca said.

"Sure," I said with a sigh.

Rebecca took off with Siren Song, who whimpered as she was carried away.

Poor Pepe. He looked so sad. He would miss

Siren Song once he was back with Caprice and Rebecca took Siren Song back to Seattle. Or maybe Rebecca would relocate to Los Angeles to oversee the production of her show. The thought made me sad. They would all be together, but I would be alone in Seattle.

I looked again for Felix and saw that he and Ted were shaking hands. I guess they had settled their differences. Then Ted put his arm around Alice and drew her close. She smiled up at him like a woman in love. Felix saw me watching them and motioned me over. Pepe came trotting behind me, keeping his eyes on the floor for any snacks that had dropped.

Ted gave me a big hug. "I'm so grateful to you for catching the real murderers," he said. "Now I'm off the hook."

"How do you know that already?" I asked. "Weren't you in jail?"

"No, I was out on bail. But my lawyer called me. He said the police were dropping all the charges. They got a confession."

"That's great!" I said.

"I really have to give you credit for not blowing my cover," Ted said. "I don't know why you trusted me. I needed to be on the set to see that the animals were OK. And after watching that last performance, I get it. Some dogs just like to perform."

"It's true. Dogs like to dance!" Pepe said.

"And thanks to being on the set, I met Alice. She's going to join PETA and help me make sure that the animals we rescue are healthy. And I'm going to work with her, taking care of abused animals."

"I love a happy ending," said Pepe. "This is as good as *Paraiso perdido*."

Chapter 36

Caprice came rushing up. She was carrying Princess, who had been completely shaved by the groomer to remove all of the tar. Without her fluffy coat, her sturdy little white body made her look almost like Pepe. Even her ears were bare, but unlike Pepe's pointed ears, they were round like those of a mouse, and she still had two little tufts of brown fur that stuck up on the top of her head.

"Geri," said Caprice. "I don't know if I can ever really thank you enough for saving my Princess, but this is for you."

She handed me an envelope containing a check. I pulled it out and looked at it. It was made out in the amount of $10,000.

"Oh, Caprice!" I said. "You don't—"

"Of course I do," she said. She favored me with a glowing smile. "I gave the same amount to your boss, Jimmy G."

At the sound of his name, Jimmy G came

strolling over with a paper plate loaded with food.

"Small reward for what you did," Caprice told me, taking my hand in hers.

"Well—"

"By the way," Caprice asked, "how did you figure it all out? Your boss told me that the murders and the kidnapping of the dogs were connected—and something about a package delivery and an independent film. But I still don't understand."

"It's complicated, but I'll try to explain it as best I can," I told Caprice.

"Start with Nigel St. Nigel's murder," Pepe told me.

"All the murders were committed by the kidnappers," I said. "Nigel St. Nigel was the first."

"But why?" Caprice asked. "Why would they kill him? Did he have a dog?"

"Actually, yes," I said. "They had kidnapped his dog, too. Rodney Klamp said Nigel didn't have a dog, but he did. Evidently this Nacho character came to the soundstage on Sunday to pick up the ransom from Nigel. But Nigel refused to pay. They got into a fight and Nacho killed him."

"But how did he get onto the studio lot?" Caprice asked. "You have to have business here to get into the studio."

"Hollywood Parcel Service," said Pepe.

"They created a fake delivery service," I explained. "Said they had a package that had to be delivered and signed for, and got onto the lot that way. The packages weren't really important. They were just an excuse to get into the lot. They used the same ruse two other times—on Wednesday when they delivered a package for me and on Thursday when Jake was killed."

"Why would they kill him?"

"I don't think they meant to. I think Jake saw Nacho taking off with Siren Song, and he tried to stop him."

"But Siren Song was never missing. She danced in every performance."

"That was a look-alike."

"But not a smell-alike," said Pepe.

"So when Rebecca refused to pay the ransom, they needed to kidnap another dog. That's when they took Princess," I told Caprice. "Jennifer probably just handed her over to them."

"Unlike the first time," said Pepe.

"What?" I asked.

"My own Jennifer!" said Caprice. "How could she do that to me? How did she ever get mixed up with those horrible people?"

"They were working on a movie together," said Jimmy G. "Nacho was the director. He had just graduated from film school. Rodney wrote the script. And Jennifer had the leading role."

"What does that have to do with kidnapping dogs?"

"They ran out of dough. It was their big dream, and they weren't going to let anything stand in the way of them finishing it. So they started kidnapping dogs—important dogs belonging to important people, like you," Jimmy G said.

"I was the first," said Pepe.

"They figured they'd get the loot to finish their film that way. Almost worked. The dirty rats just didn't count on Jimmy G."

"Or *me*!" said Pepe. "Or you either, Geri," he added.

"Well, I'm ever so grateful!" said Caprice, turning to go.

"What do you mean you were the first?" I asked Pepe.

"I remember now. It happened to me! I was walking with Jennifer when a big van came by and they threw me inside. I hit my head and all of it has been a big blank until now."

"Are you talking to your dog, Geri?" Felix asked.

"Yes, he's telling me he was kidnapped, too."

"Oh, poor little guy," said Caprice, stopping in her tracks.

"They put me in a little box. They left me all alone." Pepe was shivering. "But I got out. I broke free." His voice got stronger. "I was making my way home. Step by step. I stopped to get a bite to eat and visit with a pretty senorita. And the dog police grabbed me."

"When was that?" Caprice asked.

Felix looked at me. I looked at Pepe. Pepe looked at Caprice.

"I think it was when he lived with you," I told her.

"What?"

"I think this is your dog."

"Um, Geri . . . ," said Alice.

"Actually," I said, hardly hearing my own voice, "I'm sure he's your dog."

"What?" Caprice looked back and forth between Pepe and me.

"*What?*" echoed Pepe.

"Yes," I said. "It's true." I took a deep breath. "Pepe has an identification chip. Alice scanned it and the results conclusively proved that he belongs to you."

"Nobody told *me*," said Pepe.

"Really?" Caprice stood, frozen in place as she gazed at Pepe. "How could that be?"

"I don't know how," I said. "Jennifer probably had something to do with it. But it doesn't matter. All that matters is, he's yours and you should have him."

Felix grabbed my hand and squeezed it tight.

"Just a *momentito*," said Pepe. "Geri!" He looked up at me, his big brown eyes growing as moist as my own. "I do not wish to leave you."

I couldn't help it. My eyes flooded with tears. "You *have* to," I told him. "You belong to Caprice." I pointed at her. "But I'll always love you. *Go*."

Pepe locked his eyes on mine. He remained silent, which he never was, and just kept looking into my eyes. I couldn't stand it. I had to look down. When I finally looked up, he was ever so slowly walking toward Caprice, head down and tail between his legs.

I turned away, fearing I would collapse or cry out. Felix gathered me into his arms.

The next thing I knew, I heard a little voice saying, "Geri!"

I opened my eyes and saw Caprice right in front of me. She had Pepe in her arms.

"No, Geri," she said, tears streaking her face like my own. "Pepe is yours. He belongs to you now. I know that."

Pepe practically leaped into my arms and snuggled against me. I rocked him like a baby.

"Caprice—" I started to say.

"I love my Pepe," she said, patting Pepe gently on the head. "But I have Princess Pepe now." She picked up her little Papillon and rocked her in her arms. "I realized just what Princess meant to me when I thought I'd never see her again. Geri, it's obvious how much you and Pepe love each other. You must keep him." She paused and wiped away a tear with her free hand. Then she turned, said, "Now we each have a precious dog to love," and quickly walked offstage.

I dropped to the floor with Pepe. I sat cross-legged, and he bounced up and down, licking my face each time I kissed his velvet forehead.

"Golly," Jimmy G told me. "This is touching, just like in the movies. Jimmy G's happy for you, kid. He's even happy for the little rat-dog."

"Dry your tears, partner," Pepe told me, doing his best to dry them with his tongue. "There is *nada* to cry about," he added. "We will never be parted."

"So touching!" said Miranda Skarbos, who had emerged from the crowd like an apparition, her gray hair standing out around her thin face, almost as if she had been struck by lightning. "I was drawn to your energy from across the room. The connection between the two of you is wondrous."

"Yes, it is," I said, picking up Pepe and getting to my feet.

"I really would love to train you to be an animal psychic," she said. "Right now, what do you think he is thinking?"

I looked at Pepe. He looked at me.

"Could it be?" I was afraid to say it.

Miranda could not wait. "He's thinking of food!"

"How did she know?" said Pepe with amazement. "Maybe she *is* psychic!"

"And look what I found!" Jimmy G had gone off, and now he reappeared with the famous missing package, the one that had caused so much trouble. "It was here all along."

Jimmy G shook it. It made a rattling sound.

"Iowa!" exclaimed Miranda Skarbos, one hand going to her forehead.

"Iowa?" asked Jimmy G.

"What is in Iowa?" Pepe asked.

"*Corn!*" Miranda yelled, both hands now touching her forehead. "Yes, corn! Powerful emanations of corn are coming from that package. And something else! I cannot quite discern what it is yet."

"It is cheese," Pepe told me. "I can smell it from here."

"Cheese?" I asked.

"Cheese?" asked Jimmy G.

"Yes!" said Miranda. "It is cheese I am sensing!"

"Open it up," I told Jimmy G. "Let's find out what's in it."

Jimmy G tore the package open and looked inside. "For crying out loud! It's just a couple of bags of Nacho Cheese Doritos!"

"I knew it!" said Pepe. "I was right all along!"

Acknowledgments

We have so many people to thank for inspiration and support.

In the inspiration column, up at the top, is the charming Chihuahua known as Pepe Fitzgerald, and Shaw Fitzgerald, who adopted him, thus bringing much joy and amusement into our lives.

In terms of influence, we must acknowledge Judy Schachner, whose writing about Skippyjon Jones, the frisky kitten who thinks he's a Chihuahua, influenced our Pepe's vocabulary; Judi McCoy, author of the charming Dog Walker Mystery series, for showing us the comedic possibilities in dog-human communication; and the creators and cast of *Psych!*, the TV show that gave us a character name we couldn't resist in Nigel St. Nigel (plus hours of amusement).

In the area of support, we are grateful for Team Pepe: Michaela Hamilton, our editor at Kensington, and Stephany Evans, our agent at FinePrint Literary Management, and all of the folks at Kensington and FinePrint who helped make this book a reality. We appreciate the members of our writing group—Linda Anderson, Rachel Bukey, and Janis Wildy—for thoughtful feedback and

Elliott Bay Café for providing us with a congenial place to meet. The regulars at the Shipping Group—Cynthia Hartwig, Janette Turner, Jenny Hayes, Theresa McCormick, Mary Oak, Carol Pierson Holding, Adrienne Ross Scanlan, and Judith Gille—offered accountability and enthusiasm. Judith also helped out with the Spanish (any mistakes that remain are ours because we didn't take all of her good advice). For years, Faizel Khan has welcomed us every Tuesday afternoon to Café Argento and been not just a fan but an advocate for our work. Most of all, we wish to thank our family members, Shaw and Stephanie, for listening to our problems, suggesting solutions, and making it so much easier for us to immerse ourselves in the world of Pepe.

The fun continues
in the next Barking Detective Mystery . . .

THE BIG CHIHUAHUA

Coming soon from Kensington

Turn the page to read a sneak preview . . .

Chapter 1

"Do you think our boss will like it?" I asked my dog as I reached into the backseat to grab the framed newspaper clipping.

"It does not matter what I think," said Pepe with a bitter tone in his voice. My small white Chihuahua was sitting in the passenger seat. "I am just a dog."

"Yes, but a dog that talks," I said.

"But, *que lastima*, you are the only one who can hear me," Pepe said. "If only I could have spoken to the reporter, I would have set him straight."

He was referring to the story that had been published in the *Los Angeles Times* under the headline SEATTLE PI BUSTS DOGNAPPING RING. I had cut it out and framed it for our boss, Jimmy G, the PI in question. The article, which I'd read more than once, went on to describe the dognappings and murders that occurred when we were in L.A. a few months back filming the pilot for *Dancing with Dogs*. It paid particular attention to the famous actress, Caprice Kennedy, whose pet Papillon, Princess, was the most prominent of the dogs taken and held for ransom. Jimmy G was featured in the article, while Pepe and I were mentioned mostly in conjunction with winning the *Dancing with Dogs* competition. I didn't much care, but it galled Pepe that he didn't get any credit for bringing down the bad guys.

"Maybe we'll have better luck with this new case," I said. "Jimmy G said it's perfect for us."

We had parked right in front of the run-down brick building where Jimmy G has his office. It's on the edge of downtown Seattle in a somewhat seedy neighborhood, which suits Jimmy G fine, as he likes to think of himself as a hard-boiled detective of the same ilk as Philip Marlowe.

The building always seems to be empty. I've never run into anyone in the lobby or while walking down the hall, although there are signs on the frosted glass doors advertising the offices of a tax preparer, an importing firm, and something called Secret Star Productions. The office of the Gerrard Detective Agency is on the third floor at the end of the hall. There was a new sign, obscuring the familiar gold letters spelling out GERRARD DETECTIVE AGENCY. It was a paper sign with bold red type at the top. As I got closer, I saw it was an eviction notice.

"What is that, Geri?" asked Pepe.

"It says that Jimmy G has three days to pay his rent or else he will be kicked out," I said, pulling the note off the door. I set the framed article down and tried the doorknob, but it was locked. Jimmy G had never given me a key, despite the fact that he insists on calling me his Gal Friday. I rattled the doorknob and knocked on the glass pane. To help me, Pepe uttered a few of his tiny barks.

"Hey, don't blow a gasket," came a muffled voice from inside. I heard some banging sounds, some shuffling sounds, and then the door turned, revealing a rumpled Jimmy G.

I had always suspected that Jimmy G slept in his office, and his appearance seemed to bear that out. He eyes were bleary and red, and his white shirt was wrinkled. He was still buckling the belt on his tan slacks, and his shoulder holster and gun were hanging on the coat rack by the door, along with his fedora and tan trench coat. He smelled like cheap bourbon and cigar smoke.

He had big brown eyes that were almost as soulful as Pepe's, which may be why I am so tolerant of his bad behavior. He looked like he needed someone to take care of him, which is my weakness. I had adopted Pepe from a local animal shelter when I read about all the Chihuahuas who were being flown up to Seattle from Los Angeles, where they were being abandoned in record numbers.

"Look at this!" I said, slapping down the

eviction notice on his desk, which was piled high with papers.

"Read it to Jimmy G, doll," he said as he reached into his desk drawer to pull out a bottle of Jim Beam—mostly empty, I noticed. He took a slug, threw back his head, and gargled, swallowed, then shook his head like a dog that's wet and said, "Ah, that's better!"

"Well, this is not!" I said. I had totally forgotten about the framed article, which I had left outside the door. "It's an eviction notice."

"Oh, Jimmy G thought he heard someone at the door early this morning," he said. Jimmy G always talks about himself in the third person.

"Well, you have plenty of time to get caught up," I said. "This three-day notice is usually just a warning. As long as you catch up on your rent within three days, they won't proceed with the eviction." I knew something about the real estate business because I had worked as a stager before the housing market crashed. That's when I applied for and got the job working for Jimmy G. I took it on a lark, thinking it would do until I found something else, but six weeks later, I was hooked. Not the least because my dog loved being a PI.

"No can do, doll," Jimmy G said. "Jimmy G is a little low on the moola."

"What happened to all the money you got from Caprice?" The Beverly Hills starlet had given both me and Jimmy G a reward for rescuing her previous Papillon from the dognappers.

"All gone," he said. "Jimmy G owed some money to the wrong kind of guys. If Jimmy G hadn't paid up, he would have been sleeping with the fishes."

"I told you, Geri," said Pepe. "We should start our own agency."

"Hush," I told him. "I need to get trained by a licensed PI."

"Speaking of that," said Jimmy G, "I just got a notice about renewing the agency license, too." He began tossing the papers on his desk around. "It's around here somewhere."

"Well, you need to take care of these bills," I said.

"That's why I have a Gal Friday," he said.

"How many times do I have to tell you? I am not a Girl Friday."

"Administrative assistant?" said Jimmy G with pathos in his voice.

I have to admit the politically correct term sounded ridiculous when he said it.

"Neither. I am a private investigator in training," I said. "And we have to clear up these bills so we can keep the agency going." Which reminded me about the framed clipping I had left out in the hall. I went to get it and propped it up on one of the little wooden chairs across from Jimmy G's desk that were there for prospective clients. "Especially since the agency is in the news."

"Speaking of which, that's how Jimmy G got his new case," said Jimmy G.

"The one for me and Geri?" Pepe asked.

"The one for me and Pepe?" I asked.

"Yes, that one. The client heard about the dognapping case and called up Jimmy G."

"So who's the client?"

"A man named Mark Darling. His wife has joined a cult, and she won't respond to his phone calls or messages. He wants us to get her out."

"So why us?" I asked.

"Because it has to do with a dog," said Jimmy G, beaming.

"Really?" Pepe's ears pricked up at that.

It's true we had solved our first and only case, which had to do with a dog, but again, it wasn't really on purpose. It was more like we created enough havoc so that we got the results we wanted by accident.

"I hope it involves a bitch," said Pepe.

I was about to chide him when I realized he meant a female dog.

"With a strong aroma and luscious fur," said Pepe.

"I thought Siren Song was the one for you," I told him. Siren Song was an attractive golden Pomeranian. Unfortunately, she was down in Hollywood with her owner, and Pepe's heart was hurting.

"*Sí*, Siren Song has my heart," said Pepe. "But a dog can have many loves."

"Siren Song?" Jimmy G asked. "No, the dog's name is Dogawanda. Have you heard of him?"

"Sure," I said.

"I have not," said Pepe.

"He's an ancient warrior dog who speaks through a channeler, a woman by the name of Sherry Star. He has quite a following," I told Pepe.

"Crazy folks!" said Jimmy G, shaking his head.

"Not so crazy," said Pepe. "I think all humans could learn much by listening to dogs. I would like to have a following myself."

"So what do you want me to do?" I asked Jimmy G.

"First you have to meet with this Mark Darling. But the idea is for you to go undercover in the group. Try to make contact with the woman. Deliver her husband's message. Should be simple." Jimmy G rolled his eyes. "Unless you fall for their line of BS."

"Don't worry, Jimmy G," I said. "I'm too smart to fall under the spell of a dog."

"Ha!" said Pepe. "That is sarcasm!"

Chapter 2

Mark and Tammy Darling lived in a perfect little Craftsman bungalow in the Ravenna neighborhood of Seattle, a charming older neighborhood full of small homes set back on leafy streets. It was the sort of home I dreamed of owning, and maybe I could afford to move up, now that I had the reward money from Caprice and the prize money from *Dancing with Dogs*. The house had a roomy front porch with fat pillars and wide stone steps. A little gabled window peeked out from the steep pitched roof.

The front yard looked like an English garden, with its profusion of old-fashioned flowers: hollyhocks and ruffled irises, speckled foxgloves, and the bright blue of delphiniums. Mirrored ornaments set here and there sparkled in the sun, and a glass globe drifted in the waters of the birdbath, an iridescent bubble. Along the fence on the property line, fruit trees had been espaliered. The finishing touch: a cute little red Smart car in the driveway.

A winding brick path led us through the flowers to the front door. The porch was furnished with a swing and draped with a colorful serape. A wind chime hanging from the porch roof tinkled faintly. Pressing the doorbell triggered a sonorous chime and the appearance of a rumpled man.

"Come in! Come in!" he said. "Oh, I'm so glad you agreed to help me."

Mark Darling had worried brown eyes behind wire-rimmed glasses and brown hair that stuck up in odd tufts all over his head. I couldn't quite tell if this was due to his running his hands through his hair or if it was an artful effect achieved with a hair product. It gave him a youthful appearance, though I judged him to be in his early forties, about a decade older than I am.

A little dirty-white terrier-poodle mix came bustling up as soon as we crossed the threshold. She had a big patch of fur missing on one flank.

"That's Fuzzy," said Mark, ushering us inside. "She's been so distraught since Tammy left, she's chewing her own fur off."

Fuzzy and Pepe began sniffing butts and doing that weird jumpy dance dogs do when they're uncomfortable with each other.

"Can I get you anything to drink?" Mark asked, hurrying us through the hallway, past a spacious living room, and into the kitchen, obviously recently redone. The kitchen counters were poured concrete colored to a golden hue, and the backsplash was made of translucent leaf-green tiles. Open shelves displayed a collection of orange, yellow, and green Fiestaware plates and bowls that made me envious. "Coffee? Tea? Lemonade? Water?"

"*Gracias*," said Pepe, trotting over to Fuzzy's bowl and slurping down the water. He finished up with a mighty sneeze. For some reason, Pepe always inhales some water when he's drinking. Fuzzy sat nearby looking forlorn as Pepe turned his attention to Fuzzy's stainless-steel food bowl.

"Ugh!" said Pepe, turning away after a few mouthfuls. "Bargain brand." He shuddered and shook himself off as he does when something upsets him.

I asked for tea and Mark turned on a stainless steel kettle that was sitting on one of the burners. The kitchen was immaculate, I noticed. There were no dirty dishes in the sink. No stains on the stove. It didn't look anything like my house.

"Do you have a cleaning service?" I asked.

Mark looked startled. "Oh, you mean because the house is so clean?" He shrugged and looked a bit embarrassed. "I guess I got a little carried away. Cleaning is what I do when I'm feeling anxious."

When the water was hot, he poured it into a clear glass carafe and invited me to join him at the breakfast nook on one end of the kitchen. The windows looked out on a backyard that was even more precious than the front yard. Raised beds full of luxuriant vegetables. A huge state-of-the-art stainless-steel grill on a cobbled patio. Even a bread oven set among herbs. Stairs led up along the side of the garage. A fuchsia in a pot dangled from the eaves. It looked like there was a separate living space up there with overhanging eaves and big windows.

Mark saw where I was looking and said, "My photography studio." Then he sighed and settled back in his chair. "I haven't been up there since Tammy left."

The sky had been getting increasingly darker and as we watched, the rain began to fall, dripping from the edge of the eaves, spattering against the windows. Pepe jumped up on the bench beside me while Fuzzy lay down on the floor at Mark's feet, putting her head on her paws with a deep sigh.

"Poor Fuzzy," said Mark, taking a sip of his tea. "She's just been moping. I can't believe that Tammy would abandon her."

I found it odd that he wasn't thinking of himself, but maybe he was the kind of guy who always thought of other people first.

"Is Fuzzy particularly attached to Tammy?"

"Yes, I'm more of a cat person. But Tammy had always wanted a dog. As soon as we signed the papers, she went right out to the shelter and came home with that mutt." He took a sip of his lemonade. "I can't believe she could just walk away from her. And all this." He waved his hand at the yard. It certainly looked like a little bit of paradise.

"So how long have you lived here?"

"Five years."

I mentally computed that. They bought just as prices for houses were still going up, so they were probably watching in dismay as prices fell.

"And how long have you been married?"

"Our anniversary is June twenty-fifth. Next week. Seven years of married bliss." He took a sip of his tea and looked out the rain-smeared window at the garden.

"Do not speak, Geri," said Pepe. "That is good interviewing technique."

Actually, I wasn't going to speak anyway since I had just helped myself to one of the giant sugar cookies Mark had placed on the table and my mouth was full. The cookies looked and tasted like they were homemade. Was Mark baking as well as cleaning to compensate for his loss?

"I know what you're thinking. That's what the police said. The seven-year itch. She got tired of being married and ran off. But, believe me, there was nothing wrong with our marriage. I mean, we had our share of problems, but we were working on those."

"Ask about the problems," Pepe suggested.

"If you don't mind my asking, what were the problems?"

"Well, of course, that's why you're here," he said. He leaned forward and looked at me with those worried brown eyes. "We wanted children, but we couldn't get pregnant. No matter what we tried, and, believe me, we tried everything. Then, finally, just when we gave up, Tammy got pregnant. She was so excited."

He paused, rubbed at his eyes. "She had a miscarriage in the fifth month. It was terrible. She couldn't get over it. That's when those people got a hold of her."

"The Dogawandans?" I asked.

"Yes, she attended a seminar, and they filled

her head with nonsense. Said it was all meant to be. The baby was not gone but living in a different dimension. And she could be there, too, if she divested herself of all attachments. She was even talking about getting rid of Fuzzy. She went away for a weeklong retreat at their lodge, which is in the mountains somewhere near Cle Elum, and she never came back."

"How long ago was that?" I asked.

Mark sighed. "Almost a month ago."

"And the police aren't concerned?" I found that hard to believe.

"No. Not after I showed them the note."

"What note?"

He set down his cup, reached into the back pocket of his jeans, and pulled out a worn wallet. He opened it and pried out a piece of much-folded paper. He handed it to me without comment and watched as I unfolded it, carefully, because it had been folded and unfolded so many times it was about to fall apart. The message was written on pale green, lined paper, the kind you find in steno notebooks, like the one I carry for my case notes.

"Read it out loud, Geri!" ordered Pepe.

So I did. It read:

I'm not coming home.
Don't try to make me.
This is the last time you will hear from me.
I am dead to you from this point forward.